GOD CLOBBERS

I despise Poe Ballantine. He's obviously stolen his style from Carson McCullers. You know, I never forgave her for that nonsense at Yaddo. The "I Hate Truman Club," indeed. This boy who names himself after a cheap Scotch reminds me of her. And he thinks because he gives me short mention traipsing onto the set of the *Tonight Show* that I'm going to be *easy* on him? Squirmingly affected? I never squirmed a day in my life. God, he and Carson, two peas in a pod. — TRUMAN CAPOTE

I doubt if Truman ever read *God Clobbers Us All*. He was the same at Yaddo. A whirlwind of egoism and self-promotion. I *loved* this book. I've handed it down to Eudora, who will probably rate it a scandal. Truman was the one who stole from *me*, by the way. —CARSON MCCULLERS

Now if I could've written a book like this I might still be a famous Cuban marlin fisherman. For the record, it was boredom and the fiction of success that ended my days. The *Life* photo and the Nobel Prize were merely laurels on a dead man's chest. The writing lost its life before the writer ever did. Don't ever let them buy your soul. — ERNEST HEMINGWAY

Surfing? LSD? From which European suburb does this man hail? — WILLIAM SHAKESPEARE

Wallace Stegner handed me a copy of *God Clobbers Us All* the other day, and for the first time since 1963 I was glad that I was dead. I read this book in one sitting over at Jeffers's place under a Monterrey pine. I don't feel so alone anymore. I'm happy to see the tradition of great Western writers continue. — JOHN STEINBECK

[*sentence unintelligible*] —WILLIAM FAULKNER

The thing this novel is *about* is always there. It is like a church lit but without a congregation to distract you, with every light and line focused on the high altar. And on the altar, very reverently placed, intensely there, is a deaf cat, a powdered lemon cake, a letter to Deborah Kerr... — H. G. WELLS

I must agree with Eudora on this one, though it surpasses most of the "literary" novels I've suffered through during the last thirty years. The *atmosphere*, however – I must give him credit – put me back in the sultry, summery mind of Andalusia, with the sun setting, the scent of mimosa, and the peahens dozing in the trees. — FLANNERY O'CONNOR

Poe Ballantine, unlike the majority of his contemporaries, can write a sentence. I'm a little lost on the radio reference, but flattered nevertheless. "Write from mood," I always said, and Mr. B. apparently agrees. Tell him to lay off the booze and stay away from that shitpot Hollywood if we are ever to see him in such fine form again. — F. SCOTT FITZGERALD

The only obligation to which in advance we may hold a novel, without incurring the accusation of being arbitrary, is that it be interesting. Mr. Ballantine's Divine Punishment breaches no appointment in this regard. Print it as it stands—beautifully. — HENRY JAMES

First-rate instincts. Compelling voice. The door-slamming Pat Fillmore will go down as one of the great characters of the twenty-first century. —ALDOUS HUXLEY

I'd like to give Poe Ballantine some advice. The public is a dumb beast. Give it a pretty face or a literary movement and it will follow. I don't see the necessity of any more than one draft. —JACK KEROUAC

We'd just love to have Mr. Poe at our table. I promise to keep Bob at bay. Oh, and tell him to bring some of those round pecan cookies dusted with confectioner's sugar, do you know the ones I'm talking about? —DOROTHY PARKER

POE BALLANTINE

GOD CLOBBERS US ALL

A NOVEL

HAWTHORNE BOOKS & LITERARY ARTS
Portland, Oregon

Hawthorne Books
& Literary Arts

P.O. Box 579
Portland, OR 97207
hawthornebooks.com

Editorial:
Michelle Piranio,
Portland, Oregon

Form:
Pinch, Portland, Oregon

Printed in China
through Print Vision, Inc.

Set in DTL Albertina.

9
8
7
6
5
4
3
2
1

Library of Congress
Cataloging-in-
Publication Data

Ballantine, Poe, 1955–
God clobbers us all : a novel
/ by Poe Ballantine. –
1st American pbk. ed.

p. cm.

Summary: In a San Diego rest home in the 1970s, eighteen-year-old surfer-boy orderly, Edgar Donahoe, struggles along until the night he and his best friend become responsible for the disappearance of a fellow worker.

ISBN 0-9716915-4-1
(Trade Paperback)

1. Missing persons–Fiction.
2. Nursing homes–Fiction.
3. Drug abuse–Fiction.
4. Adultery–Fiction.
I. Title.

PZ7.B19925Go 2002
[Fic]–dc22

2003017796

With affection to the fabulous Urdang sisters.

Thanks to Cristina D. Hughes and Don Ismael for help with my atrocious Spanish.

GOD CLOBBERS US ALL

Behold, I shew you a mystery;
we shall not all sleep, but we shall all be changed.

I CORINTHIANS 15:51

PART I

Irresistible Tijuana Martini

1.

May 16, 197–

Dear Deborah:

The sky was so blue today. I had a nice long walk and bought a lemon cake at Food Basket. Lemon cakes with the powdered sugar always remind me of the four weeks Rodney and I spent in Arlington after Father died. When I learned that your father had passed away when you were fifteen too, and then I read the interview where you compared yourself to a Jersey cow, I knew we could be friends. Well. The marigolds are in bloom. It was so cold this winter I thought they might never come up. Mr. Garringer, one of my patients at the hospital, says you can grow anything in California. It must be true. I watched you again last night in Eternity. My landlord, Winston, loves that movie too, such a kind man. Once when he came for the rent, he stayed for a few minutes to watch part of This Gun For Hire. I don't think much of Veronica Lake, though I do like Alan Ladd. A man's height should not have bearing on his career. I had the strangest dream last night. It was Jean Harlow again and when I woke up I knew Rodney was here. The ladybugs always stir when he comes. I seem to have thousands now. Perhaps too many, but I can't tell Winston and I must leave the lights off and the curtains closed or he'd bring the pest man. I've circled all three of your pictures in the guide for this month. Switzerland must be wonderful this time of year. I hope you begin to act in films again soon, as I am unable to see you on Broadway. My best to Peter. I look forward to talking with you again soon.

Your devoted friend,

Beverley Fey

2.

HELEN THE ANSWER WOMAN MARCHES THE HOSPITAL AISLES sixteen hours a day, stopping only to eat or when a nurse flags her down for medications. She moves with the steadfast gait of the mountain hiker, slightly pitched to the left, her cotton diapers sagging, her head tipped so far over you can see that one day it will simply fall off. Frequently, the day aides dress her in the garb of her previous existence, a La Jolla socialite.

Though certain Latin terms have been applied, her diagnosis remains as much a mystery as her destination. Her husband, a portrait of intense crestfallen bafflement and anguish, visits once a week. An educated, affluent, intelligent woman is one day making plans on the phone for cucumber sandwiches and Jamaica tea with the Opera Club, and the next moment she is gibbering obliviously down the aisles of a convalescent hospital, a load in her drawers. Helen recognizes no one, not even herself. I usually put her to bed last, so she will be good and tired and not inclined to climb out and resume her march.

At 9 p.m. I find her chattering at Beverley Fey in the ward at the west end of the hospital. Bev, thirty-seven, is a recluse, the original Lemon Acres Nurse's Aide. The number on her time clock actually reads 01. Pocked, thick, and anteater-faced, with a slight limp, I imagine she must have had a horrible disease as a child. Her chopped, reddish, bouffant hair appears to be self-cut with scissors. Though perpetually embarrassed and eager to fade into the woodwork, Bev is the consummate aide. If the hospital held an Employee of the Month competition, it would have a wall full of only Beverley Fey photos. She wears a white severely starched ankle-length uniform dress with the kind of clunky white highly polished thick-soled shoes you would expect to see on a polio victim. Though her forearms are broad, she is still stronger than she looks. She is holding Mr. Sinelfi, a disabled stroke patient whom we call Mr. Logy because he produces a gallon or more of mucus a day, in the air with one arm while she straightens his sheepskin.

Helen babbles at Bev with her head tipped over and her slight mustache twitching. Most of her word parts are composed of the sound "fur." "Fur-in-fur," she says to Bev, hands on hips. "Fur-furfee-dee-fur."

Bev smiles at Helen, sets Mr. Logy down, dabs his lips with a washcloth, folds the sheet crisply back over his chest, and produces a cookie from her pocket.

Helen accepts the portion-control institutional Chips Ahoy package and stares at it as if it were a miniature Phoenician sundial, turning it over in her hands.

"Hello, Bev," I say.

Bev, startled, turns, pressing palms against thighs. "Oh, hello, Edgar. I didn't see you come in."

"I'm going to need a lasso here pretty soon to catch her," I say.

Under that magnificent trunk of a scar-riddled nose, Bev's wilted rose-bud of a mouth breaks into an anguished yellow smile. She swallows diffidently. Bev is my mother's age. Though I work practically side by side with her eight hours a night, four or five times a week, I seldom see her except at parties afterward, where she will suffer quietly in a corner with her unfinished glass of wine or Jack and Coke waiting for someone to drive her home. I don't understand yet Bev's withdrawal or her Florence Nightingale dedication to her job. I watch her unwrap Helen's cookie. If Helen were Bev's patient, I imagine she would be in bed now, snoring tenderly and dreaming about decaying logarithms or ribbons of Oscar Mayer smoked ham. Helen begins to munch serenely on her cookie.

"You forgot to say trick or treat, Helen," I say. "How long has she been here?"

"Oh, just a few minutes. She's all right." Mr. Logy begins to cough, working up some good goobers. Bev sops them up with the damp cloth as they come. Hutchins, the head nurse, will be in shortly to connect him to a jar so that he can sleep without drowning.

Bev studies me with her tiny drooping gray eyes and begins to fidget with a thermometer cover. The only way I can ever get her to converse with me is to talk about patients or old movies.

"I saw *From Here to Eternity* last night on KTTV," I tell her.

The sad gray eyes light. "So did I," she says, pouring a glass of water and holding it to Mr. Logy's lips. He seems tranquil now, like a babe in its mother's arms. "Did you like it?"

I don't want to disappoint Bev, but what can you say about an old movie where the high point is two people smooching in bathing suits on the beach? And there was a commercial every four minutes, Ralph Williams, Ralph Williams Ford, in the Beautiful City of Encino … "It sure was better than the book," I say. "I liked the ending."

"Oh, the ending is wonderful. I must've seen it fifty times."

"Fifty?"

"Oh, forty or fifty, I don't know. Maybe sixty. As many times as *The King and I*." She touches her ruffled ostrich hair and her cheeks flush slightly. She seems out of breath with that fluttery enchantment that you only see in her when she talks about her movie stars. "That was Deborah Kerr's twenty-first movie," she says, stroking Mr. Logy's head. "Not counting the first one, *Contraband*, where she got cut out. Joan Crawford was supposed to play Karen Holmes but she didn't like the costumes. Eli Wallach was going to be in it too, but Frank Sinatra got that part. You know the scene where he's shaking the dice? Those are really olives."

"Olives?"

"Yeah, it was his screen test, but it was so good they just kept it in. Do you know that Deborah got six academy award nominations but never won? That's the most times anyone's ever been nominated without winning." She shakes her head. "It isn't fair."

"I never paid much attention to Deborah Kerr," I say. "Is she still alive?"

"She retired from films in 1969. But she's acting on the stage. I think she'll make movies again."

"You must really admire her."

"Oh, gosh, yes." She clasps her big bony hands. "Have you seen *Black Narcissus* or *The Chalk Garden*?"

"No, I haven't."

"Oh, you must see them," she says. "I have a movie guide ..."

Helen has lost interest in her cookie. She seems to want to talk about Deborah Kerr too. "Fleebie fleebie, doo-fuffy fur," she offers, enthusiastically.

I have not seen Bev talk this much since I brought up Clark Gable at a party two months ago. I wish I could stay and talk with her. Watching her come to life is like watching the bloom of some rare tropical orchid— but Mr. Logy has begun to gag and now Helen, flagging, has dropped her cookie and turned her attention to me.

"Well, I'd better get her to bed," I say, retrieving the pieces and pocketing them. "She'll fall straight over in a minute."

Bev, suddenly self-conscious, grazes her ear with an index finger. "Yes, I know."

"Thanks again for the cookie, Bev."

"Furfee fur…" says Helen in farewell.

I lead Helen back to her room, which she shares with the Swamp Lady, an insensate skeleton tied to her bedrail to keep her hands out of her feces. Helen is an easy patient, compliant and eager to converse and please, still the perfect hostess. She babbles all the while I undress her, her eyes seeming to express and understand, her head cocked to the left like a songbird.

I remove her nylons and shoes, shuck her blue-striped dress and brassiere, pitch her diapers in the corner, and sponge the urine from her legs. Helen still has a decent body, firm and flush. I don't believe she has ever had children. She must be in her early fifties. Her feet are lumpy and wide from the thousands of miles she has logged since she landed here in her Fabulous New Realm. We talk about the weather, tropical fish, a weird movie I saw at the Ken Theater recently called *Lemonade Joe*, any subject is all right. I've been feeling filthy and low the last three months. I counsel with her about my mixed-up life:

"It didn't seem wrong when I started …"

"Furdlee-fur."

"She hates her husband anyway."

"Hutha-hutha, hur-in-fur," she answers, eyebrows raised, as if I should've known better from the beginning.

"No need to scold," I say. "I know it's wrong. And I'm going to break it off soon, very soon."

"Oh, sure," she says.

"I'll tell her tonight. I know you don't believe me, but I will. I just wish I had another girl. Is that too much to ask?"

Helen winces as I scrub her pudendum. I never imagined in my life I would be scrubbing anyone's pudendum. I dust her backside with baby powder. "Yeeees," she says. "Oh, yes. Gleebie-dur-dee-fer-infer."

"Of course," I grumble, as I toss the washcloth into the corner with her diapers. "You're right. But how many billions of women are there in this world, and why can't I just have one I can introduce to my mother and take to the movies and not have to drive out into the boondocks looking in my rearview mirror the whole time to end up on a putting green with?"

"Fer-doodle-dee-der," she replies confidently.

She wears a grimace as I fasten a fresh pair of diapers over her hips and swaddle her in yellow pajamas with red robins, fat cartoon worms in their beaks. She wriggles and scolds me in her fur language. She may, like a child, simply object to being put to bed, or she may suddenly in some way realize that a strange boy is kneeled before her in her bedroom.

"Are you tired, Helen?" I say.

"Oh, yes," she croons heartily.

I lead her to bed. "But you'd also like to walk another forty-three miles."

"Yes, yes," she says.

Swamp Lady grunts something from her prehistoric dreams. She never speaks coherently out of her bearded and withered mouth, though once after I accidentally broke her toe she rose like a vision from the underworld and called me a sonofabitch. I can smell her tarlike feces, which leak constantly out of her onto a special cotton pad. I pull up Helen's rail. She stares up at the ceiling as if it were bristling with stars. "Good night, Helen," I say. "Good night, Mrs. Swamp…"

3.

AFTER WORK THAT NIGHT, PAT FILLMORE'S TEAL-BLUE MALIBU cruises through the parking lot as I am trying surreptitiously to make extramarital arrangements with Chula La Rue, a twenty-seven-year-old Mexican aide, who has three kids.

The window of the Malibu glides down. Pat grins nubby-toothed at me from under her rug of hair cut in the style of a Mongolian rice farmer. Pat and I have been drinking companions for about six months now, ever since she escaped from Montana and became employed as a nurse's aide at Lemon Acres. She is the ruddy, gregarious sort of girl who slams you on the back in greeting and displaces your spine. Her reasons for leaving Montana are unspecified, though she, like so many others flooding into the state, has an obvious California Dream, and once she mentioned standing before a judge who said something to the effect of: *I don't ever want to see you in Bozeman again.*

She nods at me. "Hey, you horny little wetback," she says to Chula. "Bev and I are going out for a drink. You guys wanna come?"

Bev, sitting in three stripes of shadow on the passenger side, looks like a woman behind bars. Whenever I see Pat and Bev together, I think of a large, flaming planet and its distant but enthralled and ice-crusted moon. Bev has always been able to deflect any of our after-work invitations, even the Irresistible Tijuana Martini, but since the arrival of Pat, all of this has changed. Big Pat Fillmore is not the type of person to accept a simple no thank you or two. Hutchins, our skinny, redheaded head nurse, says that while on the surface Pat is trying to help Bev overcome her phobia of society, deep down she is really trying to fix her own loneliness and isolation. Paralyzed by social awkwardness for a good portion of my life, I would like to help Bev break out a little too. "Where you going?" I say.

"Diablo's," she answers. "Then Roberto's for chicken tacos."

"Sounds good," I say.

Chula kicks me in the ankle.

"But Chula says something's wrong with her battery. I'm gonna look at it. I think it might be her starter."

Pat winks at me. She knows I know nothing about cars. "Maybe you could look at my starter sometime too. Been a while since I had my battery charged."

I grin amiably, while Chula flips a bored glance up at the stars.

"All RIGHT!" Pat turns up the song on the radio and bellows along with it off-key:

Went to a dance
Lookin' for romance
Saw Bobba-Ran so I pulled down my pants...

"You're coming over tomorrow afternoon with the DICA," she says, sticking her big round head out the window. In the sodium-vapor lamp-light I can almost see the word F-U-N emblazoned in crude gothic Day-Glo letters across the upper left quadrant of her soul. "Right, Eg?"

"Yeah," I answer nervously. "I'll bring my battery charger too."

"Bring-a you DIC-A, honey. That's all I need. Ha! Ha! Hey, I'm gonna tell that one to Doctor Rigatoni. I'll talk to you all tomorrow. Day off! Praise the gourd all Friday! Don't wear off any parts!" Meaty-armed, Pat wrenches the car into drive. The window slides up to the sound of hearty guffaws. I see Bev smiling faintly as the car turns down out of the driveway.

I own a mangy chipped green 1956 Rambler American with surf racks, an oil leak, and an Alpine slide-in stereo I bought on sale at Dow. Chula clamors impatiently into it and says, "God, when she asked if we wanted to come I almost said, 'Three times.' What the hell is a DICA anyway? You're not screwing her too, are you? I didn't think so. *Chihuahua*. She wouldn't give you your dick back..."

Chula and I drive out to Lake Murray. It is a foggy May Wednesday night, the mist spinning and splashing against the street lamps. I have ended up with Chula not because I wanted to have relations with a married woman but because I found her like a box of free kittens on my front seat one night after a drunken party at Pat's house. We have been going at it for about three months now, and I am looking for a way out. I am not built for the surreptitious, high-pressure intrigue of adultery. I have a plan to go to Australia, which will solve all of my problems in one fell swoop. I have about three hundred bucks in the bank. All I need is a one-way ticket to Perth and I'll hitchhike from there. I am going to build a shack on the beach from fronds and surf and fish all day, eat coconuts or whatever they've got on the beach there in Western Australia. It's going to happen any day.

Chula sits close to me and nibbles my ear. Nurse's aides, in my experience, are the most sexually active group outside of nymphomaniacs, prostitutes, and meat packers. We also party hardier per capita than any other occupation, not only because we are poor and our futures are dull, but also because we see every night firsthand the terrible and heartbreaking things that are going to happen to us when we grow old.

I don't know if Chula is a legal citizen. She speaks mildly accented street English sprinkled with Spanish. At the age of twelve, she told me, she came to the United States from deep in jungle Mexico, losing a brother in a sewer tunnel crossing the Texas border. She hustled her way up from the bottom and was lucky in my opinion to find someone dumb enough to marry her. She has no formal education, though she knows how to slaughter and dress a hog. Across her abdomen is a polished blue scar in the shape of an elongated Z, which she alleges came from a boy who raped her with a machete down by the Lacantun River. She uses this story to threaten me, saying that she killed him with the same machete three days later when he was lying on his belly catching turtles: she cut off his head and watched it float away down the river. *You hurt me,* she likes to say, *I hurt you. You cut me, I cut you.* I have my doubts about the veracity of a head floating all by itself down a river. My opinion is that it would sink. Chula is going to be surprised one day when she walks into the lobby of Lemon Acres Convalescent Hospital and finds out that I am gone.

I slow just past the pink stucco restaurant and bait shop on Lake Murray Boulevard, the sign out front reading "Ten Rolled Tacos for a Dollar," and turn left onto the dirt road that leads to the lake. I cannot tell if the car that has been following me is her husband's 1964 Galaxie, but I am relieved to see it continue straight along the boulevard. I imagine he will circle back to try to catch us in the act. My sense is that it is not sex these days but the hunt that really excites him. He is an ex-Marine, one of these exceptional few who professes to have enjoyed his tour of duty in Vietnam. Chula is not very attractive anymore, except perhaps to a desperate, sex-crazed, and misguided eighteen-year-old orderly picking up scraps. The gravel pops under my tires as I coast through the gates of the lake.

Chula snuggles into me. She is coffee-skinned, no more than five feet tall, and her teeth are so white that sometimes in the dark they seem blue. She wears her hair teased and pulled back in two tails secured with red rubber bands. Her legs in their dark nylon skins are as hot as link sausages. She has this astounding basal metabolic rate. Her eyes behind black plastic winged specs appear to be charred from the application of excessive mascara. I intend to tell her tonight that we are through, that I have found a girl my own age and interests. I have made up a name for her: Angelica. Angelica is a timid virgin who lives with her grandparents because her parents were devoured after they fell into the hammerhead tank at Sea World. I drive around to the other side of the lake, glancing in my mirror, and park by the dam. Chula sets her winged specs up on the dashboard.

"Chula?"

"What is it, baby?"

"There's something I need to tell you."

"Oh, *nene*," she says. "Kiss me first before you go on with your philosophical bullshit. I like a boy who shoots first and asks questions later."

I turn on the radio. Chula intimidates me. I hate being afraid of a woman barely five feet tall. She begins to unzip my fly. I catch headlights dissolving in my rearview mirror. There would be no one out by the lake at this time of the morning, not legitimate fishermen anyway, only killers, drifters, dopers, and jealous husbands.

"Wait a minute ..."

"What is wrong with you tonight, *corazónsillo?*" she says.

"That car behind us."

"What car?"

"It's him."

"Who?"

"Your old man."

"That ain't him," she scoffs, turning her head listlessly.

"How can you tell?"

"What are you talking about, *hijo?*" she says.

"He's playing a game with us."

"Mike doesn't play games. If he knew about us he'd be roasting your *huevitos* now with anchos on the barbecue."

The headlights spring on again, as if cued, and the car creeps out into the road. I cower down in the seat. Chula laughs. "He's not smart enough to find us," she says.

"The guy was in *Nam*," I say.

"Relax. He's asleep. Snoring away like a little pig. He never stays up past the ten o'clock news and his seven Budweisers."

The car passes. It's too dark to see inside, but Chula's right: it's a station wagon, teens smoking weed or a couple of bottom-fish poachers looking for a spot.

I begin to take off Chula's clothes. Her hair is tough as fishing line. Naked, she smells of gardenias and popcorn and muskrat. Before I know it we are down on the seat, fogging up the windows. The ripple waves of the black and mist-locked lake below slush up and back through the pebbled shore. In the cup of Chula's throat I concentrate on a little Catholic medal glittering on a chain. I hear a car go by. I don't look up, but I know it has to be him.

4.

BECAUSE I HAVE TO GO TO LA JOLLA TO SEE NILS SAAG THAT afternoon, I drive the coastline – the fog burning off in twiny vapors like the memory of an ancient film star – until I get to Torrey Pines, a long flat state beach with a nice big parking lot and two empty lifeguard towers. Famous for its PGA course located on the piney bluffs above, the beach itself has nothing to recommend it: no physical features (reef, shelf, bar, jetty, or southern contour) to trip the ground swell. And the bottom conformation generally makes whatever waves that can struggle into existence break in mud-colored flops too close to shore.

But at Windansea or Tourmaline Park or Marine Street or any other gravy breaker beach, I and a thousand other otter-brained sea harlots would be fighting over every last wave like a bunch of old ladies at a department store bargain bin, and all I want today is to be left alone, and to scrub my dirty soul in the sea.

The parking lot is empty. My only company is a few golfers up on the bluff, who chuckle, swat, tap, and waddle away like a gaggle of Charlie Chaplins in their hundred-dollar International Business Machine slacks. It's a cool early morning, a slight onshore breeze. The fog has lost its daily war with the sun. The water is unusually clear. I can see the distinct undulant filigree of kelp blossoming in their beds in the pale green distance. The no-more-than-three-foot-high waves are lifting and folding onto the beach like the automatic steps in the down escalator at Sears. The waves sigh as they sizzle drearily up the shore. I unstrap my board from the rack and slowly make my way down the sand.

I fiddle around in the small, bumpy waves for a while, nestling into the curl, cutting the edge, kicking back out. The water is cold, no more than sixty-five, but it feels good. I don't wear a wetsuit or a leash. I've got an old homemade eight-four board I picked up at a garage sale in Oceanside. The guy said it belonged to Phil Edwards, though I know Phil liked balsa and this one is filled with Styrofoam and no one is going to knowingly sell a Phil Edwards board, used or not, for twenty-five bucks. I like the bigger, older, round-nosed boards over the lighter, new needle-nosed variety. I've washed off a lot of sin and melancholy in this blue elixir called the Pacific Ocean. I ride a bit harder and take a couple of deliberate scrubbing tumbles over the sand, but it still doesn't help.

After an hour or two the breeze switches offshore and starts holding the waves up. Even in a small breaker you can pick up quite a bit of speed when it holds up and hollows out. Most of the rides are inside, but they keep setting up out there, big rolling swells that never form, and I keep paddling out like a sucker to meet them. On the drive down I heard on the radio that a tropical storm from Mexico was on its way to bring some big surf, who knows, maybe even to the Great Plains of Torrey Pines State Beach.

The sun climbs above the bluffs. I lose track of time. I float out past the breakline, sitting on my board, the waves popping and shushing behind me. I think about my stalled, crooked, and directionless life. I need to move out of my parents' house. They want me to go to college. But I can't resign my fate at this early stage to becoming a sociologist or an English teacher or a respiratory therapist. Why don't I have the force of character to be something dynamic, like an actor or an underwater sea explorer? Why, while I was spending all those years on the couch eating Corn Doodles and watching reruns of *Gomer Pyle*, didn't I learn to play the guitar? Every guy I know who plays the guitar has a nice-looking girl…

A devil ray, at least eight feet across, flaps along blindly under me in clouds of boiling silt. Then, out beyond the kelp beds, five or six pewter blue and pink dolphins suddenly breach all at once into the baubles and dimes of sunlight. Australia is the place to be, I think. When complication is the problem, simplicity is the answer. I make a resolution to call a travel agent first thing in the morning about one-way flights to Perth.

Now all at once golf balls are raining all around me. I turn to see silhouettes of men in knickers at the top of the bluff. I can make out the glints of their teeth and the shiny plates on their clubs as they continue to crack balls at me and laugh. Or to give them credit: perhaps they are only duffers who for once in their life would like to hit something they aim at, like the Pacific Ocean.

Whatever the case, I know it's getting late, so I paddle back to shore. The beach is suddenly populated by writhing oil-smeared bikini-clad girls, pot-bellied children poised attentively with plastic shovels over castles and one-foot assays to Hong Kong, and a hip pale-faced couple in green sunglasses roasting hot dogs over a ring fire. Two guys slide across the last shallow glaze of low tide on round, homemade plywood skimboards. A green-eyed dog, part shepherd, flings itself out of the back of a van, romps down the sand, and blasts into the surf.

The lifeguard, Jay, whom I know from high school, steps out onto his platform and shouts down to me, "Hey, Edgar. What are you doing out here? They got bigger break out at the bay!"

"They ain't bad!" I shout back to him. "Every now and then I like the paddleboat rides!"

He nods and shows me his big white teeth. A body builder, bowed-out stiff and gleaming brown as a pretzel, Jay wears a boxy pair of sunglasses and a jacket of wet zinc on his nose. Jay was popular in high school, first to be invited to the keg party on Cowles Mountain or Fiesta Island and always fighting off the girls. Anyone who knew me in high school will tell you – who? Edgar who? But I know Jay from the Regional Occupational Program. We were in hospital assistant class together and saw dead people and lanced each other's fingertips to type our blood and smoked pot in the back of the bus on the way to volunteer sessions at the VA Hospital. Jay worked for a while as an orderly at Beverly Manor on Lake Murray Boulevard before he got this job as a professional suntan and girl watcher. I don't think it's possible to drown at Torrey Pines unless you tie a boulder around your neck.

"Hey," says Jay. "You hear? There's a tropical storm coming up from Baja. Six to eight!"

"I heard," I cry, putting up my thumb.

"We're driving up to San Clemente in the morning," he says.

"I gotta work tomorrow afternoon," I shout up to him, even though I know he's not inviting me. "I'll probably go to Abb's."

"All right." He raises his hand. Women have begun to flock around the column of his tower. He smiles broadly. "Later, dude."

NILS SAAG LIVES ON CAVE STREET IN THE POSH BUT CROWDED and sterile community of La Jolla in a quirky thirteen-level mansion of his genius architect father's design. I park inconspicuously down the street – Nils is sensitive about appearances – and walk up the hill through the tall iron gate and to the giant, arched double front doors where I ring the bell. From his eagle's-nest bedroom window thirty feet above, I can hear Neil Young raging through the screens. *Hate was just a legend, and war was never known …*

I ring the bell again. At last a smooth, haughty face framed in long, glossy brown hair appears in the top window. It might be Neil Young himself. The face nods. The music goes off. In another minute the door opens.

Nils is twenty, a slender lad with quick-moving heavily browed eyes, shiny shoulder-length hair, and small delicate hands, the nails of which he manicures carefully but does not cut. He is wearing floral bell-bottoms, a stiff beige high-collared ecclesiastical frock, moccasins, and a neckful of Celtic charms. Between his feminine fingers smolders one of those clove cigarettes hand-rolled by orphans in Pakistan. "Hey, man," he greets me indignantly. "You said two o'clock."

"What time is it?"

"It's after three."

"Sorry. I lost track of the time."

"Where you been?"

"Ocean."

He grunts. "You look like a drowned rat. Come in." He pecks at his cigarette. "Let's go out to the garden."

I follow him through the curious mansion with its odd wall angles, jutting indoor porches, Moorish arches, switchbacks of black-carpeted stairs, International House of Pancake sashes, and tiles of rose and blue-bottle tinted glass. Chrome-framed prints of the revolutionary icons of our day glower down over us through their beards among the scent of carpet glue, beach breeze, burning clove, and a sweet fleshy odor like bing cherries and fried baloney. My stomach growls. Through the great west bay window hangs the burnished purple ocean with hard glimmers on it like dental mirrors and a group of islands in the offing that may well be Hawaii. Though I know he has parents – because once I saw his mom, looking like a magazine cutout, rattling a sterling silver shaker at the wet bar in the piano room – Nils seems to always be alone in this glamorously eccentric and colossally lonesome palace.

Nils demands a certain ritual from me. (He is lonely, doesn't get out much, and I suppose he does this with all the people who come to do business with him.) We sit by the garden. I am required to call the high-quality LSD he sells "pure." We must sit and talk like medicine men about Nietzsche, Nostradamus, or Kahlil Gibran. I must defer to his ideas. He will show me a catalog of organic toilets or geodesic outhouses and I will approve. Then he will make transported statements about dolphins or American Indians, and then at last he will guide me to his room at the very top of the mansion and give me the quantity of "pure" and I will be on my way.

We tour his organic garden, as tiered and complex as his house. He seems to forget he has shown it to me three times before. The carrots and other root crops sit on the lowest level below a family of caged peppers and seven varieties of onion. He shows me the orange, the tamarind, and the barren sweet lime tree, which clatters leaflessly in the sea breeze waiting for another season. He plucks an orange and gestures at me to sit down at a redwood table overlooking the carrots.

"Should we take a little bud?" he says, producing an ornate rosewood box.

"Fine."

"It's purple Kenyan," he says, fastidiously trimming with scissors a dark bud like a tiny evergreen, layering the tacky foliage into a briar pipe the ivory bowl of which is carved into the bust of what might be Leif Ericsson, Thor Heyerdahl, or possibly Fred MacMurray, and applying fire.

The Kenyan tastes like maple syrup and a basement full of lepers in unlaundered bathrobes, and very quickly the sky is vibrating, the pressure has doubled behind my eardrums, the fruit trees are creaking conspiratorially, and my already handicapped IQ has plummeted forty-six points. I wish I were back on the ocean. Nils is nodding at me. He is one of those who nods almost constantly as if he knows and understands all and everything is cool, brother. I stare at the lacy waving tops of his organic carrots and watch the way the sun gleams from his perfectly center-parted Neil Young hair, which is so gleaming and clean-looking I think he is definitely using a conditioner.

"Pretty good bud, eh?" he says.

"I'll say." A fly lands on the back of my hand but I don't have the energy or the organization to wave it off.

"So what if we've had other lives before," Nils says, lifting his palms. "What good is it if we can't remember them?"

"I couldn't remember them anyway."

"No, the answer is: because if you could remember them, then it would change the life you're living now."

"I think I see what you're saying. One day you get to view all your lives like a rack of Halloween costumes that you can't remember ever having worn …"

"Yeah," he says, peeling his orange slowly with his long pointed fingernails. I remember reading something about Chinese aristocrats who grew long fingernails to demonstrate their independence from labor. "Kind of like that. Except you'll remember them then. And all your lives on earth will be done. You want an orange?"

Though I'm actually starving and my mouth feels like one of Davy Crockett's old coonskin caps, I don't want to commit to anything that prolongs my stay. The barren sweet lime tree rattles its agreement in the breeze. I wonder what day it is. I feel flensed like a quivering block of Eskimo whale blubber. The sun is already beginning to set over the top of colorful Saag Mansion.

"No, thanks," I say. "I'll stop by Jack-in-the-Box or something on the way back."

"Jack-in-the-Box!" he roars. "How can you eat that crap?"

"The Jumbo Jack is pretty good," I reply weakly.

"It's all SHIT," he says. "Frozen dead animals from factories in Illinois. You ever seen the guys that drive those trucks? Zombies, man."

I've seen those trucks. I could drive one of those Jack-in-the-Box Zombie Trucks. I could make three thousand bucks in one summer. I could live like a king in Australia. I scratch my mop of snaggled, salty hair. I should've at least brought a Coca-Cola with me, but he might not have let me in with it. Nils pops an organic orange segment into his mouth. A squirrel chatters at us from the top of the fence.

"Do you ever notice how closely the calls of the squirrel and the dolphin are?"

"No."

"Listen."

I take another toke from the pipe and tilt my ear. "Yeah, maybe," I concede.

"Dolphins are more intelligent than people," he says.

Certainly right now they are. I wonder why I smoke marijuana. It makes me so nervous and DUMB, and now I have to drive fifteen miles home on the freeway with a bunch of LSD in my car...

"So are pigs," he adds.

I rub a knot on my forehead and try to figure out where it came from. "If a pig played checkers with a dolphin," I propose, "who do you think would win?"

"Both of them are too intelligent to play checkers. Only humans are stupid enough to play checkers."

"You're right there," I say, lighting a Marlboro. Nils glances at it with disdain. His argument is that if you smoke something nonorganic that isn't rolled by lepers or orphans in Pakistan then it should get you high. My argument is that nicotine is a perfectly legitimate and natural euphoric – it DOES get you high – and it has the large advantage over purple Kenyan of not turning your skull into a bowl of butterscotch pudding. "I've never really liked checkers ..." I say.

"Now, Nietzsche, you know what he said about checkers?"

"I don't recall."

"You don't remember the quote from *Zarathustra*, 'I teach you the superman'?"

"I never finished *Zarathustra*. Did I give it back to you?"

"Yes. You didn't finish it?"

I blink my cherry eyeballs. "I didn't understand what he was talking about. I read his biography, though."

Nils snorts.

I doubt if Nils understands Nietzsche either, outside of a quote he read on the side of a box of chamomile tea.

"Nietzsche is aphoristic," I say. "He has no methodology."

"You don't know anything about Nietzsche, man," he retorts, handing me the pipe. "Nietzsche is a genius, man."

I hold the pipe until it goes out and then I return it to him. I don't tell him Nietzsche lived with his sister and spent his last years in an insane asylum trying to stuff an ice-cream cone into his right eye. I remember a quote, something like: "The thought of suicide is a great comfort ..." *Is this responsible philosophy?* I want to say. *Is this the fruit of a lifetime of love of knowledge?* And who can abide any philosopher who opposes beer?

Nils dumps the spent contents into his garden, trims a fresh bud, and repacks the pipe. "It's getting cool," he says. "Global cooling," he adds. "The ice caps are spreading. Another ice age is coming. The earth will be out of petroleum in twenty years. It's the end of the reign of man. And good riddance, is all I have to say ..." He lights the pipe and engorges his lungs, his cheeks caving in, his inflamed eyes assiduously focused on the combusting herb. Nils hacks and splutters for a while, blasting out long plumes of expensive African smoke. He offers me the pipe.

"No thanks," I say. "I gotta get going pretty soon."

"I don't have much time for philosophy these days anyway," he says. "I'm getting into Buddhism. It's all an illusion," he says, sweeping his arm across the sky.

"Then we don't have to worry about the ice caps," I say.

"Don't you wonder about that, though?" he says. "Where you'll go when you die?"

"I'm going back to the ocean," I say. "What about you?"

"On," he says, looking up fondly at the cloud-rippled sky.

"I've got to get going," I say. "I have to see a girl."

Certain words are teenage magic incantations. Ocean. Girl. Beer Keg. Neil Young Concert. Even possessive aristocrats like Nils have to let you go when you invoke one of them. "OK," he says, reluctantly. "Let me just show you this organic toilet I'm going to order. If everyone in the United States had one of these …"

I hurdle down the left lane in my Rambler, top end seventy-five miles an hour, the door of my glove compartment rattling, paint chips flying off my hood. I am late. I seem always to be late these days. There are new freeways everywhere in preparation for the millions soon to arrive, but there are no rush hours in San Diego yet, except an occasional clog around Waring Road, which clears out pretty fast once you pass San Diego State University. I haven't eaten anything all day except a bowl of Cap'n Crunch and an English muffin with peanut butter, and my blood cells are crying out for something rich like lamb chops, coconut cupcakes, and a quart or two of dark brown beer. The skin of my face is ceramically glazed from the stringent burn of sun and salt, and my eyes are piggy little blots of scarlet. I try to shake the fog of the purple Kenyan. I check the rearview mirror for cops. Maybe Pat will have a jar of vacuum-packed dry-roasted peanuts in her cupboard. Definitely we will have some beer and some "pure." As I speed up and around and down the Fletcher Parkway exit I am pleased to see the left turn light on Baltimore Drive turn green like some kind of benevolent sorcery before my eyes.

5.

MY BEST FRIEND PAT FILLMORE IS A BLACKFOOT INDIAN OF twenty-five years who stands around five foot six and weighs in at two hundred pounds. In front of discouragingly sparse crowds this spring, I watched her play women's semi-pro football at Balboa Stadium until she bruised her spleen and had to quit. A few years ago, she took third in the Montana State Women's Arm Wrestling Championship. Pat is a Capricorn, though she will be the first to emphasize to you: Sagittarius rising. She lives by herself in a large, breezy, one-bedroom Marengo Drive apartment, which for a nurse's aide making a dime over minimum wage is only made possible by the generous checks she receives from the government for being an Indian.

Entering quietly without a knock, I find her slouched in her hairy plaid couch, muttering drowsily under her cap, one burly arm laid up along the wall, her big shot-putter's legs crossed, her face a vivid, high-blood-pressure crimson. Pat likes to talk about a future in hotel and restaurant management or possibly an advanced nursing degree, but neither of these is likely to distract her any time soon from her true mission in life of stumbling through the door of the party that never ends.

She holds up a pebbled pink-glazed tumbler and stares at me in a haze of wonder as if I am Robert Peary just returned against all odds from the blizzards of Northern Greenland. On the counter next to a bag of cheese puffs is a pink puddle in the middle of which sits a nearly finished half-gallon jug of Gallo rose. There are dishes piled in the sink and the smell of hot dogs, Top Ramen, scrambled eggs, and Pine-Sol.

"What *happened* to you?" she squawks.

"I went to the beach."

"Son of a beach," she says. "You should've *called* me. I was *worried*. You said you were coming over this after*noon*."

"It is afternoon."

"But it's *late*. I started drinking *wine*. Look, I almost *finished* it. I thought you got *arrested*. What were you doing at the beach, *surfing*?" She ejects the word from her lips as if it were a worm. "How come you didn't come get me? My goddamn leg is asleep." She climbs out of the couch and stumps around arthritically until she is standing at the counter in front of me, wine bottle in hand. She is wearing a quilted Jackie Stewart denim racing cap, a baggy bright purple parrot shirt, Wrangler cutoffs, and thick red flip-flops. Her toenails are painted candy-apple red. She dribbles the last of her Gallo into the tumbler and says, "Did you buy the DICA?" DICA is our code word for LSD, ACID spelled backward.

I produce the sheet from my wallet and flourish it like Thomas Jef ferson after penning the last dot on the Bill of Rights. "Twenty hits," I say proudly. "Nils says it's the best he's ever had."

"What kind is it?"

"Clearlight," I say.

The only drugs Pat got to try up in Montana were Wild Turkey and Marlboro 100's, but she has been making up for lost time. Now to her counterculture *Easy Rider* résumé you can add mari-hoochie (as she likes to call it), psilocybin mushrooms, and the popular pill form of working-class Dexedrine commonly referred to as white-cross tabs. "What did we have last time?" she says.

"Orange Barrel."

"Is this as good?"

"This will make Orange Barrel look like Johnson and Johnson baby aspirin."

She presses her hands together prayer fashion under her chin. "My TURTLE died."

"It is the most powerful LSD of all time," I add. "It will make you forget what geological epoch you are in."

She tips back the last of her wine, her lower jaw and tongue extended so as not to miss a drop. "I don't even know what geological whatever you call it I'm in NOW," she declares, wide-eyed with a cackle. Her hot asthmatic gurgle of a laugh is infectious. "Can we drop now?"

"Are you sure you want to?"

She cuffs the back of my head. "Why wouldn't I?"

"Coyote dogs might steal you and carry you off to raise you in the hills."

"That happened once to my cousin Burfie. We never saw him again, except once I think he knocked over our trashcans ..."

The Clearlight, or Four-Way Windowpane, as it is sometimes called, comes in gelatin tabs about the size of your eye pupil that are embedded into a sheet of aluminum foil and intended to be divided into four doses, hence the term "four-way." I like a double dose myself, half a tab. I don't mind forgetting my geological epoch. I snap one of the tabs in half on a cutting board in the kitchen with a razor blade.

We swallow the minuscule chips of potent amber and immediately drive to the liquor store for beer. Pat is a fascinating person to me, not only because she was raised barefoot poor on an Indian reservation in a highly restricted and conservative environment with only Perry Como on the radio, but also because she can buy booze. She has three older half-sisters, none of whom she has seen in fifteen years. They, since the long-ago disappearance of her father and more recent death of her mother, are the extent of her family, the memory and mood of which often leaves her quivering with a desperate and unquenchable loneliness that erupts into full-blown fits of par-tee fever, which is precisely where I am at in my development, having just hatched from the soft larval stage of suburban puberty into the bright lights of a cultural revolution whose script was written by horny old men for bored First World teenagers: seek pleasure unabashedly, reject all authority, distrust any wisdom not from a foreign country, sha la la la la la live for today.

Our bizarrely harmonious friendship is marred only by her radical alcohol-induced personality changes, her tendency to brawl, and the gloomy, misanthropic women who occasionally appear at her door, especially Carol, an attractive young artist who draws pictures of naked women with militantly rendered clitorises in the shape of either crucifixes or women's symbols. Carol always gives me the nervous feeling she is flirting with me in a way where I will end up in a closet with a pair of scissors in my chest.

By the time we get back to Pat's Marengo Drive green-shagged one-bedroom apartment with the Maxfield Parrishes on the walls and the hairy plaid furniture and all the plants hanging Babylonian fashion in crocheted nets from the acoustic ceiling, the world is already crackling at the edges and we are beginning to flush and grin and lose eye contact.

Pat wrestles with the grocery bag, trying to extract the beer. I grab a handful of cheese puffs. "Why do you feel dirty in your soul?" she says, ripping the tab off a tall Coors and licking at the hump of foam like a camel at a button of salt.

"Chula," I answer, crunching away on the cheese puffs. "Gimme one of those beers."

"You need to find a nice girl," she says.

"Who?"

Pat has to think, chin rested on the back of her hand. "How about Horse?" She laughs in appreciation of her wit.

I guzzle back my Coors, which tastes like water with gold flecks and faint swirls of radon. The truth is that Horse, an antisocial Lemon Acres swing-shift aide who lives in a small muddy Lakeside trailer exclusively in service to her muscular stallions, is not a bad-looking girl. Though she is easy to make fun of because of her long narrow face, sloping withers, and pronounced front teeth, I have nevertheless admired her secretly many times as she has walked away down the aisle, and I don't mind peeking into her rooms as she leans over to pull up a bedrail or yank out a bottom sheet.

"You could have your own ponies," Pat adds, whinnying at me. She traipses away, leaving me thinking about Horse, who wears these short nylon see-through dresses over her dark and perspiring muscular body. There is also something appealing about women who do not think they are beautiful. Girls who get what they want are never really pretty. I notice that my hands are orange as if I have murdered a cartoon character, and I am suddenly parched and strangling from salt as if I have dumped one of those dehydrated macaroni-and-cheese packets down my throat. I find another beer and stroll into the living room to sit down. *Life is a show just for me*, I think. And my mind is a jukebox full of scrambled and broken pop tunes. I have to sing them to set them free:

Freeze the babies, who don't have enough to eat.
Shoot the children, with no shoes on their feet.
Hose the people, living in the street.
Oh-oh there's a solution ...

Gem-eyed shadows flitter barby-tailed across the walls. I cross my legs and my knees seem higher than my head. The curtains spring to life. The sparkly-sprayed acoustic ceiling begins to hump and crawl. Pat is out on the balcony hanging over the rail singing Freddy Fender down into the bushes.

I am suddenly seized by a premonition that I will lose all my friends. I wonder if God laughed when he saw the headline: NIETZSCHE IS DEAD.

A surge of hilarity and panic begins to press in against my diaphragm and all attempts at suppressing it with beer fail. On the wall above the television set, an op-art image of a big eye stares at me. I get up and its gaze follows me across the room. Finally I have to go over and turn it around.

Pat is standing behind me, hands on hips. "What did you turn my eye around for?"

"It was talking to me."

"What did it say?"

"It said: 'Wonder Bread helps build strong bodies twelve ways …'"

She slaps her hip. "Oh, Jesus my muffins," she says. "Son of a BEE-keeper. Did I tell you? Did I lose my – swear to GOD!" She hitches up her cutoffs and swivels her head around, eyes wild in her head. "Boy, this stuff is STRONG. Phew!" She waves her hand back and forth under her chin. "How long has that song been on?"

"What song?"

"Oh, I thought the – Jesus, my muffins. Why don't you turn on the – put on some of that – " She tips her head over. "Is the phone ringing?"

"It's the doorbell!" I cry. "The milkman's here!"

"Ahhh!" she cries.

"Let's get out of here, Pat," I say. "The walls are closing down."

"Where we goin', Mexico?" Her eyes search my face. "I don't want to go to the trestles again," she says. "The last time that train almost knocked out my teeth. Let's go to Tijuana."

"It isn't Tee-uh-wanna," I say. "It's TEE-WANNA, all right? TEE-WHF-WANNA. Say that, TEE-FWANNA."

"TEE-FWA-FWA – I can't say it."

"Let's go to the beach."

"Son of a PEACH farmer," she says. "Let's boogie. Lemme change my clothes. I'm gonna wear my shitkickers. Promise me something before we go." She grips my thin arm firmly and implores me with the arched brows of a tragic silent-screen star.

"What is it?"

"Say you won't leave me."

"Why would I leave you?"

"I have fear of ambamdum – andbandom – however you say it."

"Abandonment."

"Yes, that too." She gulps from her Coors. "Promise me."

"OK, I promise you."

"Swear to me to God on a Bible."

"I swear to you to God on a Bible."

"Not a bubble. A Bible."

"That's what I said, a Bible."

"Do you have a Bible?"

THE DRIVE IS TREACHEROUS. CHROMIUM BUMPERS STREAM in the fever-green sun as the hard razor-jelly sounds of cars whisk past. My eight-four board is still strapped to the rack, casting a shadow over us like a ridiculous sombrero. Sometimes you can drive OK on acid. Sometimes you can do things better on acid than you can in real life. Playing caroms, for instance, or answering trivia questions about the Seven Dwarves. Dock Ellis of the Pittsburgh Pirates pitched a no-hitter on acid against the San Diego Padres in 1976, the only no-hitter he ever pitched. I feel all right behind the wheel, except I am in danger of forgetting where I am. I have to sing:

Each night before I WET *the bed, my Bay-*BEE.

Whisper a little PRAYER *for me, my Bay-*BEE.

"We'd better not go where there are any cliffs," Pat advises. "And no train trestles."

"You're afraid of heights."

"Well, you're afraid of mice."

"I am what I am."

"You're a YAM?"

"A cop is following me."

"Tell him to bite me. Roll down your window. I'll tell him."

"No, wait a minute. I'm wrong. Thought it was an oyster but it's snot. *You've painted up your lips and rolled and curled your pubic haiiirr...*"

"What's on the radio?" says Pat. "I don't want to listen to you sing anymore." She begins twisting around the knobs on my dashboard. "How do you change the ... What's wrong with this goddamn –"

"That's the heater knob."

She explodes into laughter, snorting so hard the tears squirt out of her eyes. All that snorting breaks me up too. We almost suffocate from laughter. I look down at the speedometer and I am going fifteen miles an hour.

"Stop the car," Pat pleads, still gasping for air, her face warped in pain, tears shining on her cheeks. "I can't breathe. I'm gonna pee my pants. Where are we anyway?" she cries. "St. LOUIS? Whose idea was that?" She begins to laugh again, gulps wrong, and gets the hiccups. "Crap," she says. "I've got the hick-hick-hiccups. Crap. I need a beer. I got the – hick. Oh, goddamn it, can you please stop somewhere and let me pee?"

When we arrive at Mission Beach it is already evening and Pat has tried every trick in the book to rid herself of hiccups, including an ancient Indian remedy that never works, but finally it is almost getting run over by a longhaired old burnout grinding down the boardwalk on a huge tricycle that cures her. We sit on the cement seawall above the busy boardwalk and drink from blue-green bottles of foamy geranium-smelling Löwenbräu. The taste of the beer makes me happy. The sand is heaped like snow in twilight and smells of liverwurst and almonds. The sun plods down into the sea. The sky is grained with rubies and chocolates and pinks. Two pretty girls on roller skates sail by, leaving an exact phototaxic and chromatic replica of their trajectory. The ocean waves lift and roll, then snap off in elegant, clean, stained-glass rows. The shiny sand close to shore is paved like wet silver and the water in close is as dimpled and hazy as a sheet of scalloped lead crystal. A girl in a vaporous lavender skirt dances out into the crystal and spins.

"She's not wearing any underwear," I say.

"Neither am I," says Pat.

"Wait a minute," I say, starting to climb down off the wall for closer inspection, when a man dressed in brown gas-station rags suddenly appears to Pat's left. He is radiating danger and the smell of onions and cumin and manure. He has a nut-brown complexion with dirt in the creases of his cheeks and a beard that looks as if it is hanging by pipe cleaners from his ears.

"Have you got a pair of scissors I could use?" he says.

"What for?" says Pat.

"I need to cut my hair," he says. "These guys from the CIA are after me."

Pat studies him with narrowed eyes, as if she might've gone to high school with him and is trying to place the class.

"No, no scissors, man," I say. "Is that the cops?"

Both Pat and the grungy onion man turn.

Two sailors on skates approach from the opposite direction. They are big and shirtless and pink with blond butch haircuts. They are going too fast, and they don't know how to skate very well. You can hear them rumbling up, stiff-kneed, clacking and thumping, and they are laughing from beer.

"Oh, chup, watch –" says one.

Pat turns as the larger of the two becomes airborne. His skates are where his head should be. He seems to be floating like a talented Chinese acrobat. Pat starts to sing "Off We Go Into the Wild Blue Yonder." The earth shakes as he hits the cement. A plane passes overhead dragging a Coppertone banner and droning a B-flat. The blood shining down the sailor's legs and head does not seem real. He is still laughing.

"Oh, shit," he says.

"Oh, shit," his friend agrees.

"We should help him," says Pat.

"What can we do?"

"Give him your shirt."

I begin to remove my shirt. I will foam the last of my Löwenbräu into his wounds. But the sailors have already gathered themselves up and are rolling away, their laughter now fractured and mournful like the calls of caged whippoorwills. The splatters down the walk are not blood platelets and hemoglobin but slowly rendered brilliant "S" designs, which the new skaters streak through and which dull gradually back from crimson to sand.

The girl in the diaphanous lavender skirt continues to twirl. A few people have stopped to watch her, heads angled down for better viewing. The grungy onion man has disappeared. The smoke races and flickers out from the tip of my cigarette.

Pat leaps off the wall suddenly, flips her bottle into a trashcan, and ambles down the sand toward the sea. She moves like a dancing bear, hands striding low, palms back, her big backside swinging. The ocean is a principal fixture in her California Dream, but she is afraid of the water. A tiny tumbling chrome-clad breaker flickers up the sand after her ankles and she whirls and scampers away.

"Why don't you go in?" I say.

"Electric eels," she says, out of breath and grinning insanely. She removes her boots, rolls her pant legs to the knees, and once again tries to brave the sea. Another microscopic wave skims in. She turns and dashes away. "Tidal wave!" she cries.

Down in the distance, Belmont Park shoulders out of the mist like some old forgotten mansion. There is talk of closing the amusement park because some old woman fell off the wooden roller coaster years ago. All along the glittery shore, speckled gelatinous piles of beached silver-blue jellyfish gleam in the twilight.

"I'm going to name this one Bambi," I say, lifting one from the sand by its back and letting it hang like a great handful of translucent guts between my fingers.

"Don't give me a heart attack."

"We'll take it home," I say. "Have a peanut butter and jellyfish sandwich."

Pat clutches palm to chest. "Put it down before I barf."

"The stingers are on the tentacles," I explain.

"I didn't know jellyfish had testicles," she replies. "Which way is the liquor store?"

The seagulls topple and swing above us, whistling Doppler melodies. The terns bounce dutifully down to the first crown of creamy phosphorus. I drop Bambi the Jellyfish when someone screams through the mist from the roller coaster a few hundred yards away.

"He's staring at us," says Pat.

"Who?"

"Him. Charlie Rockingchair."

I turn to see a grinning cross-eyed pink-nosed beach rat in a green pullover sweatshirt squatted beside a cement-ringed fire.

"Hi," he says.

"Hey."

"How's it going?"

"Great."

He holds up a stumpy can of Right Guard spray deodorant. "Wanna see it blow up?"

"No," I say.

"I been blowin' 'em up all the way down the beach," he says, his crossed green eyes quivering with delight. "I just throw 'em in the fire."

"Charlie," says Pat. "Don't do it."

"My name's Robbie," he says, holding up the can. "I got three more. I stole 'em from the store."

"The cans are for your ARMPITS, Charlie," advises Pat sternly.

"I'm gonna throw 'em in the fire," says Robbie.

I watch a group of huge swells setting up far out and wonder if they'll form. They're six feet or better and they just keep building. I can feel them in my loins. That tropical storm is on its way, and I'm not going to miss it tomorrow.

Robbie grins at us cross-eyed, like Friedrich Nietzsche or a Labrador retriever with a stick in its mouth.

"Please don't blow up the can, Charlie," Pat enunciates carefully, her eyes shut. "I just had a heart transplant."

Robbie grins. "BOOM!" he shouts.

"Why does this shit always happen to you when you're tripping?" Pat whispers in my ear.

"We have to go now, Robbie," I say.

"I'll go with you," he says.

"Just wait till we get out of here, OK, Robbie? She has a BRAIN tumor, all right?"

"Hey," he says, holding up the can. "Don't you wanna hear it blow up?"

It's dark by the time we get back to the car and all the Hell's Angels are roaring down Mission Boulevard headed for Ocean Beach and my ears are still ringing from the explosion of aerosol and metal and the wheezy scrape of beach rat laughter. Two scarecrows in a rumbling purple Road Runner thunder up next to us, gawking. They have a good guffaw and roar away.

Pat twists around the rearview mirror and stares into it, running a finger along each eyebrow. "I look like Fred Flintstone. Don't I?"

"Give me my mirror back."

I miss the turn at Grand and have to go up Garnet, which has too many lights. Two pink stars blink on in the north sky. The streetlamp shadows writhe in liquid purple flows across the windshield. I light a cigarette that tastes like cow pies and valentines. The moon floats up, a big ball of yellow paper and lumber. Pat is suddenly quiet.

"Look how big the universe is," she says. "Do you believe it? Where does it all come from?"

"Baked beans," I say, confused for a moment by the presence of Mount Soledad, a mountain apparently moved here overnight and somehow instantly covered with million-dollar homes wrapped in wrought iron with FOR SALE signs planted in the front lawns.

"Beans? What are ya talkin' about?"

"The Baked Bean Theory. It's a cosmological theory about the origin of the universe."

"The who?"

"It says that at one moment in the beginning of time there was this Big Baked Bean that exploded and everything that we know, matter and furniture and chrysanthemums, came from that."

"Chrysanthemums?"

"Yes."

"I can't even say that."

"You just did."

Pat is leaned over in her seat in order to stare up into the universe, which is partially concealed from view by the end of my surfboard. "It must have been a pretty big bean," she says. "Where did you hear about this?"

"I read it in *Time*."

"*Time* magazine. Swear to GOD? Why are you so full of shit?" She leers at me delightedly. With her great Siberian moon face, deep uptilted chinks for eyes, heavy sinister eyebrows, and shag dutchboy haircut, she looks to me like a drunken Soviet prime minister. "I am spaced OUT," she cries, hands clamped over her ears. "I am tripping over the cosmetology of the universe. I had a girlfriend in cosmetology once. She never mentioned anything about baked beans. Why do you always make up this shit when I am TRIPPING? Where are we anyway? Are you *lost*?"

The interstate lights pass over us in rows of gracefully swinging chandeliers or partially mutated hurricane lanterns full of luminous but delicate carnivorous fireflies. "If I don't know where I'm going," I reply, "then how can I be lost?"

"Where are we going then?"

"Where do you want to go?"

"Mexico."

"Mexico and what?"

"Mexico and martoonis." She holds up two fingers. "Tea martoonis. And I have to pee."

"You just *peed*."

"I did?" She twists wildly around in her seat. "Where?"

"I mean before we left."

"I'll be all right. Where the hell are we? Let's go to Bev's house. 2525 Cherokee Avenue."

"I know where she lives."

"Party at Bev's," she says. "Gimme that sheet of acid."

"What for?"

"I'm gonna get Bev to take one."

"She won't do it."

"I'm going to talk her into it. She's gonna have fun for once in her life."

"She's too OLD, Pat."

"Gimme the sheet," she insists. "What do you know about it, you and your baked beans?"

6.

I FEEL LUCKY TO FIND CHEROKEE AVENUE. I FEEL LIKE COLUMBUS sliding bearded and scurvy-ridden up the gritty virgin shores of the Bahama Islands, eager to meet the Hindoos and coerce them out of some black peppercorns. My tires scrape along the curb in front of the house where Bev lives, an old sleepy Georgian divided into three palatial apartments and set far back from the street. Every window in the house is dark.

"No one home," I say.

"She's home, Egbert," Pat says. "She's always home. Come on."

We climb out of the car. Pat slams the door hard enough to tip my car over. We whisper savagely at each other.

"Are you sure the door is shut?"

"Bite my fuzarus," she says – one of her favorite sayings – then the usual lament: "Oh, if I only knew what a fuzarus was…"

We sidle up the flagstone walk past a birdbath big enough to farm trout in, and Pat begins to hammer on the door, which seems to be breathing like that door in *The Haunting* with Julie Christie. I am itchy and giggly with crystalline housefly vision, a vacuum-packed electronic bladder that is sending messages to my ribs, and a taste like lemon drops all up in my ears. The great house is surrounded by a grove of tall vanilla-smelling pines that sway gently at the tops and make a high shushing sound like the hissing of a club soda just after you mix it with Scotch. A few of the gold needles tumble down, glittering in the moonlight.

Pat continues to thump on the door and call Bev's name.

"You're going to wake all the neighbors," I say.

"It's only eleven-thirty."

"She's sleeping, Pat."

"You don't need to tell me that."

"Maybe she isn't home."

"She's home. Where else is she going to go?"

At last the door opens. Pale and tapirlike, Lemon Acres' Original Nurse's Aide Beverley Fey stands before us barefoot in the dark doorway in an ankle-length flannel gown.

"We didn't wake you up, did we Bevvie?" says Pat with infinite gentleness.

"No," she says, squinting at us in a sleep-swollen and perplexed pout. "What are you doing?"

"We came to visit you."

Bev expresses no disappointment at the fact that we are giggling, out of sorts, irrational, and reeking of beer at her front door at nearly midnight. She registers no umbrage that we have disrupted her sleep. She touches her hair and offers a timid miniature archaic smile. Her pitted face shines like wax and her grandiose nose is melting down to her pale lips like a fat gray candle. "Come in," she says.

We follow her into moonlight gloom and high ceilings and the frowsy scent of ancient wood and raspberry tea. The rooms are furnished appropriately in the heavy green Depression style. In the darkness Pat and I find opposite ends of a grand sofa that smells of cerecloth and the electricity of rain. The lights stay off whenever we visit Bev; the curtains, night or day, remain closed. Though Pat seeks Bev out regularly, coaches her in matters of society and fashion, drags her to parties and bars, gives her rides to and from work, brings her with us to the beach, Bev still seems mystified by the attention. Pat says, "Did you just get home from work, honey?"

Bev is sitting across the way from us in a large chair next to the silhouette of a table with a telephone, hands folded in her lap. "Yes," she says.

"You took a cab?"

"Yes."

"And you went straight to bed?"

Unable to discern faces, my perception dissolved by strong drugs, I feel as if we have been assigned new roles. Pat is a stern mother interested in the social development of her unpopular daughter, who mysteriously refuses to accept the invitation of the handsome team captain to attend the prom. I am a pair of cigarette-scorched lungs and a bladder full of beer attached to a curved spinal cord.

"There was nothing on TV," Bev says.

"You sleep too much," says Pat. "It isn't good for you. It isn't good for your metabolism."

"I like to sleep," says Bev.

My eyes begin to adjust to the gloom. Vaguely familiar faces begin to emerge from the ancient show-business magazines arranged in a fan across the coffee table. Bev's deaf white cat, Persia, strolls haughtily in from the kitchen, stretches, then tucks itself into a ball in a diluted nest of moonbeams on the hardwood floor.

"We've got something for you, Bev."

"What is it?" says Bev.

"It's a surprise."

"I'm not doing any drugs," Bev says.

"It isn't a drug, Bevvie…" Pat rises and moves toward Bev's chair, kneeling like a suitor. "Don't be a pooper. Tell her how fun it is, Eg. Tell her that open door thing, that Alan Huxley stuff."

"Aldous."

"Whatever. Tell her psychedelic means 'to see the light.'"

"It means 'clear mind.'"

"It's the same thing. Tell her about it, that transformation of the grubworm thing…"

"It's metamorphosis…"

"I can't say that, meta-horphamis."

"If she doesn't want to, Pat…"

"Oh, don't listen to him. I am all alone in a world of poopers. Hold on a minute, where'd I put it? Yes, now. Remember what I told you last night? Look how tiny it is. Do you know how many monkeys they can fit into one of these? Eg and I…"

Bored by the futility of Pat's crusade to convert a pumpkin into a carriage, I stand up to look outside and make sure no one is fooling with my board. I pull back the heavy green curtain. "Let's go, Bevvie Dear," Pat says. Hot Planet Pat seems to know the secrets of her frozen little crater-pocked moon. She knows that if she keeps working on Bev with her vitality and charm, eventually something will break: she will make the connection, strike that deep running source, and make it run to the surface. Once she finds that little crystal junction where the spark is set and the personality flames, the transformation will be complete.

I hear Pat whisper: "It's not like you have to worry about your *chromosomes*, honey…" Outside, the mist comes tumbling down the street in great gelid blasts like a herd of lost and fretful ghosts late for the graveyard.

Now Pat is suddenly ecstatic, dancing a jig around the room. "She took it, Eg."

"Took what?"

"The DICA."

"She didn't."

"Did."

"How much?"

"A whole one."

"A whole one? Why?"

"I couldn't cut it," she gasps in explanation. "It was too dark. She'll be all right. She's gotta catch up with us. Now we'll have us a *party*," she says, crouched with fists triumphantly pumping the air. "Put on one of those Patti Page records, Eg."

"The stereo is broken," says Bev.

"Turn on the radio then. What have you got to drink, Bev?"

"Seven-Ups."

"No, I mean to DRINK. Crap, Eg, we forgot beer. What is wrong with us? Let's go to the store."

"We can't leave her."

"Come with us, Bev."

"I'm not dressed," Bev says.

"I'll go," says Pat. "But I can't drive a stick. I can't even work your radio. I am *bongo* drums. You go, Eg."

"I can't buy beer."

"Right. We'll go together. Like the pilgrims."

"We can't leave Bev," I say.

"Bev, will you be all right?"

"I have some blackberry brandy," Bev volunteers.

"How much?"

"I don't know. It's in the kitchen."

I find the radio, a great embroidered and abandoned hunk of carved F. Scott Fitzgerald maple with knobs like steering wheels sticking out of it.

"It tastes like COUGH syrup," Pat bellows from the kitchen. "It is cough syrup."

"Turn on the lights, why don't you?"

"You want yours mixed with Seven, Eg?"

"My cough syrup?"

"You won't be able to tell the difference. Bev, you're having one too…"

Bev makes a whickering sound, pale bizarre imitation of laughter. I feel a crushing sympathy for her. I am the father of her new consciousness, I think, and I must protect her, guide her, and now "God Bless America" is suddenly running in irresistible brassy refrain through the shattered jukebox portion of my brain. I'd sing it if I knew the damn words: *through the night of the bla-bla-bla-blaaah.*

There is a sound outside like boys going by on skateboards. *Punks*, I think. *Landlubbers gonna fool with my board.* The hall light switches on. I hear singing: "When the Saints Go Marching," then a scream, then disjointed laughter. The toilet flushes. Bev is still planted desolately in her great green Depression chair.

Plane engines groan overhead.

"They found us!" shouts Pat, waving her arms.

Pat and I wait with scientific fascination for Bev's metamorphosis. Even when we get her to stay at a party, she never finishes her first drink. This should be some kind of explosion, I think, like mixing bleach and ammonia. How will she blossom when I bring up the subject of old movie actors now? This could be very fun, I think, like giving a can of beer to the family dog. The empty blackberry brandy bottle sits squarely in the middle of William Holden's forehead. A panel of light from a passing car whisks like a magic carpet across the wall. Bev sits quietly in her armchair by the telephone, patient and unchanged, half her original blackberry drink gone flat.

"Don't you feel anything, Bev?" says Pat hopefully.

"No," says Bev, smiling faintly with what I imagine as relief.

"Did you take it, Bev?" I say.

"You didn't spit it out, did you?"

"I took it," says Bev.

"What the hell, Eg," says Pat. "It don't affect her."

"I've never seen anything like *that* before," I say. "You probably didn't give it to her. You probably gave her a piece of aluminum foil …"

Pat shakes out the sheet of LSD from the front pocket of her denim jacket and counts the hits. "No," she says. "Eighteen left."

"How long's it been?" I say.

Pat tries to check her watch. "What time is it?"

"It's one-thirty," says Bev.

Pat's stubbornly vivacious face melts into sudden horror. "One-thirty!"

"Yes."

"Oh, my Jesus, we have to get more BEER. Come on, Eg. You stay here, Angel. Eg and I are going out to get some more beer. Now don't you go back to *bed*. We'll get this all straightened out. We're going to have us a *party*…"

7.

BY THE TIME WE RETURN TO BEV'S APARTMENT, THE DRUGS ARE beginning to wear off. "Look," says Pat, as we climb out of the car. "The lights are off."

"They were off when we left."

"Yes, but now they are OFF!"

"I fail to see the distinction."

Pat begins to hustle up the walk, the bag full of beer jingling against her chest. "Something is not right," she calls back to me. "Look, the door is open. Did you leave the door open?"

"I don't remember. Be quiet, will you?"

"We shouldn't've stayed so long. We should not have bought all these beef snacks."

Pat rips open the screen door. I linger back. The air smells of warm cement and wet grass. It is the time of morning when even the insomniacs doze. Pat sticks her head back out the door. "She's not here."

"What are you talking about?"

"She's not *here*."

I hurry up the walk.

Pat says, "Something was wrong the minute we drove up, I could tell."

"Turn the damn lights on, will you? Why do we have to do every blessed thing in this house in the dark?"

"The radio's off," says Pat. "Did we turn the radio off?"

"She probably went back to bed."

"After a whole hit of Clearlight?"

"Check the bedroom."

"Yes. Bev!" she calls. "Bevvvieee!"

I stroll into the kitchen and switch on the light. Persia, the deaf white cat, glares at me from the countertop, then hops down and skitters past me. I hear Pat's boots clomping down the hall, doors opening and closing, the floorboards creaking under her weight. Her voice rings with anxiousness: "BEVERLEY? BEVERLEY FEY?"

When I turn on the living room light, I am shocked to see the walls teeming with shifting, gleaming ladybugs. There were never any ladybugs when I was here before. Maybe she is breeding them, I think, sending boxes of them to florists in Oregon. Bev's half-finished drink is still on the telephone table. The empty brandy bottle is still sitting on William Holden's forehead.

"She's not here!" Pat bellows.

"Bathroom?"

"Not here."

"What the –"

"Shit."

Pat, all business, emerges at the head of the hallway. "Come on, we've got to find her. This isn't funny."

"She probably went to visit a neighbor."

"She doesn't visit her neighbors."

"She got a little scared."

"Maybe. Come on."

"Where are we going?"

"We'll split up. You go out back. I'll check around front. Then we'll spread out from there…"

"Is there a note anywhere?"

"Jee-Zuss."

"Bevvie… Bevvie?"

I find nothing out back but pine trees, a pair of tilted, rust-scaled clothesline poles, and a cyclone fence woven with whispering ivy. Out front the streetlight is pulsing off its moth powder in a soft clockwise glitter. Pat is squatted on her haunches examining the sidewalk.

"Lose your gum?" I say.

"Look at this," she says. "What is it, footprints?"

I squat next to her. "Could be. Hard to tell in this light."

"They are," she whispers ominously. "It's blood isn't it?"

I twist my head around, staring at the shapes. They could be footprints. They could be infrared maps of Burma or Uruguay.

"The left foot, isn't it?" she says. "She stepped on a piece of glass."

Pat and I follow the footprints until they disappear into a neighbor's front lawn.

The skateboarders, I think. *The landlubbers took her.*

"Let's go look for her. She can't have gotten far."

We hop into my Rambler, drive around the block three times, widen our arc, slowly pass trees, stop in front of lit windows. Hedges mingle with shadows from the long sheets of oily yellow streetlight. Emerald-eyed cats peer out at us from grease puddles under cars. Turning a corner, I glimpse in my mirror the faint image of a woman in white climbing into a strange car, but it can't be Bev, I think. She would not be that careless or bold. Roberto's, the nearby Mexican stand and only restaurant that Bev likes to frequent, has been closed for hours.

We return again and again to Bev's unexplainably empty apartment. When the dawn breaks we cover all of East San Diego, looking for a woman in a long white gown. We drive downtown. We walk through Balboa Park. At nine o'clock that morning we are sitting in Bev's living room again. The ladybugs have begun to stir. They shift like a great metallic skin on the wall, then a few break and buzz in lazy reconnaissance like little motor-boats through the air.

"Where did they all come from?" Pat says.

"Bev probably didn't have the heart to kill them," I say. "You know they're good luck."

"Good luck," she repeats glumly.

"She'll show up," I say feebly.

Pat grinds her palm into her forehead. "Why does this shit always happen when you TRIP?"

"We'd better get out of here," I say.

"What are we going to tell everyone?" she says. "She has to work today. Oh, God, Eg." She buries her face in her hand. "What have we done?"

PART II The Slender-Horned Adulterer

8.

I NOTE COMMOTION AS I PUSH THROUGH THE MAIN DOORS of the hospital. At the front desk an attractive aide I do not recognize seems about ready to break into tears. Hutchins, the skinny, carrot-headed vegetarian head nurse, crooks a finger at me. *It's about Bev,* I think. They've found her dead, torn to pieces on the freeway, an unexplainably high dose of LSD in her bloodstream. The police want to talk to me. I summon what little energy I have. My nose is running and my head feels like a plywood box hammered full of two-penny nails.

"What's going on?" I say.

"Mr. Joliet has expired," she says.

I am relieved. Bev is all right, after all. She showed up to work somehow. She was hiding in her bedroom closet the whole time, waiting for us to leave. I look around and think I see her turning the corner. "Who is Mr. Joliet?"

"He was admitted yesterday afternoon. He expired this morning. Apparently the day aide did not check him." She wrinkles her nose in disdain. "He's been dead for several hours," she adds.

"He's not mine?" I say.

"No," she says. "It's an unfortunate situation. Mr. Joliet's family will be here in an hour. This is Norma Padgett." She indicates the pretty new aide. "This is her first day at Lemon Acres. Norma, this is Edgar Donahoe. Mr. Joliet is her patient. Normally, I'd pair her with Linda, but we're two aides short tonight, and Mrs. Fung is getting a Foley plus they moved Watkins to Disturbed. He attacked Marguerite and broke her glasses about an hour ago. It's been a hectic day. Mercury's in retrograde, you know." She twines her skinny red fingers together. Hutchins is a dyed-in-the-wool hippie with hairy legs and a Volkswagen van, but I notice she wears a wedding ring. She is also an excellent nurse, compassionate and competent and modern in all her medical attitudes except for that part about Mercury. She gazes benevolently upon Norma Padgett, the very good-looking new aide who is either pale by nature or blanched at the prospect of preparing a man who has been dead for several hours.

"I'm afraid this isn't a particularly warm welcome, Norma," she says.

"A dozen donuts would've been better," I say.

Norma laughs as if she is going to be sick. Her lashy eyes are lush and very blue against the pallor of her face and the brunette frame of her feathered-back shoulder-length hair.

"Who called in?" I say.

"Pat," she says. "And she says Bev won't be coming in either."

"Oh, really," I say, feigning surprise.

"I don't know what could be wrong with Bev. She was fine yesterday. She hasn't called in sick since I've known her. She's worked here since the hospital opened, you know."

"Yes, I know."

"Our best aide," says Hutchins to Norma. "You'll get to meet her. Very shy but wonderful with her patients. We actually have relatives on admission day who request her care."

I continue to nod. My head might be full of balloon gas. "Let me make a quick bed check," I say. "Then I'll meet you back in Mr. Joliet's room. Say ten minutes."

"OK," says Norma timidly.

"I'll show her the room," says Hutchins. "It's section B. 116."

"Don't start without me!" I call gallantly.

Norma Padgett, arms folded across her chest, is waiting for me outside the dead man's door. I have a good close look at her. Though her hips might be the tiniest bit wide, her face is flawless, like a maiden in a Botticelli painting, with a high regal forehead and those big rainy blue eyes. She wears a new white uniform that seems almost Victorian with its pink swatch of lace at the collar. She smiles at me as if someone has stabbed her. I notice that her front teeth are slightly crossed.

"Ready?" I say.

"Not really," she says.

"This your first hospital job?"

"Yes."

"Where'd you work before?"

"Nowhere."

"Not anywhere?"

"No."

"How old are you?"

"Nineteen."

"You look older, I mean younger. I mean you look good…" I prop a hand on my hip and marvel for a moment at the independence of my mouth and brain. "Where did you go to high school?"

"Helix."

"I went to Henry."

She nods.

"Have you taken any hospital courses or anything?"

"No." She flicks her hair off her shoulder with the back of her fingers. "I was going to but they hired me anyway."

"Right, that sounds about right. OK, well then, we'd better not keep him waiting," I say, pushing open the door and thinking: *Ask her out non-chalantly, while you still have the advantage. Do not waste time. Element of surprise. A woman of this caliber will be lost with hesitation. Women of this caliber cannot stomach wishy-washy men; they want swashbucklers, bikers, criminals, smooth and aggressive orderlies…*

We enter the stench-filled darkness and I flip on the light. What awaits me sends all my shallow machinations veering suddenly south like honking geese bound for Central America. I have seen many dead patients, prepared half a dozen in my year of training and employment among the "convalescent." But this thing piled in the corner that was once called Mr. Joliet is utterly new to me, unholy and bizarre. He is actually sitting up in bed and glaring, one arm raised overhead as if in greeting. I might still think he was alive if it weren't for the shiny rigidity of his features and the overwhelming tropical-fecal smell that permeates the air. No wonder the day aide left him. She didn't forget to check him. She opened the door, saw him like that, closed the door, clocked out, and quite sensibly decided to never work in a convalescent hospital again.

"Lordy," I say under my breath.

Norma stands behind me like a reluctant child meeting Santa Claus or Mickey Mouse for the first time. "What's wrong?" she says.

"Nothing," I mumble. "I see they've moved his roommate down to the ward. That's good."

Norma peeks around me. She moans and lays a hand over her forehead. "Why is he like that?"

"Mercury in retrograde?"

"I've never seen anyone dead before," she says.

"Close the door," I say, glancing from the corpse to my wrist. Normally I wear a watch to track pulse and respiration, but in the pandemonium of the last twenty-four hours I left it in my glove compartment. "We'd better get started," I say. "We've got forty-five minutes to fix him up. You know, the family has to come in and have a last look."

"Right." Her expression is a freckled cringe.

I move to the corpse. What we need now is a little joke to ease the tension. If the corpse and I could perform a ventriloquism routine, for instance: *Hey, get me out of here willya, I'm late for the bingo game.* But my mind is as dry of wit as a communist bookstore, and I still have not accustomed myself to the brutal ghastliness of his appearance. It looks as if he has been poisoned or electrocuted or tortured to death. Gnarled in the sheets, his right knee hiked up like a hurdler's, his eyeballs bulge out of a head that is already a skull. His mouth is a puckered, side-slung hole. Somewhere in the throes of his final moments he managed to discard all his clothes. A pair of his underwear is slung across the lampshade on the bed stand. Like many patients who die suddenly, he has evacuated his bowels into the sheets.

I pull his chart from the hook at the end of his bed. "They admitted him with pancreatic cancer," I say, "but cancer didn't kill him." I lay my ear to his icy chest. "Probably MI. Heart attack. Looks like he died of anger."

Norma remains at a good distance, her arms locked across her chest. "Looks like he's still angry."

"I don't think he liked it here."

"I wouldn't like it here, either."

"No," I agree.

I begin to untangle the sheets from his legs. His skin is the color and temperature of two tablespoons of molasses stirred into a glass of iced lemonade. Slathered in a loose mess across his legs and sheets, his feces look like green refried beans. "The first thing you have to do before rigor mortis sets in," I recite, "is try to fit back in the dentures." I glance at the glass on his bed stand where his bubble-decorated teeth float. "In this case, rigor mortis is long established."

"If it were any more established you could put him in a wax museum."

"Yeah, or on a pole in a cornfield."

"I don't understand how the girl in charge of him could leave him like this," she says.

"The day shift people all have chromosomal defects," I say.

"It shouldn't be our responsibility."

"Well, War Nurse will get her on Saturday."

"Who's War Nurse?"

"She's the battleship who works on the weekends."

"How much undertaker work do you do around here?"

"Everybody who comes in here dies, but sometimes they last for years. We'll be here one day too. In some societies they take the old ones and leave them on a mountaintop or float them out to sea in a boat. In this society, well here we are…"

She stares at me as if I have said something profound. Now is the time to ask her out, but I grow discouraged suddenly realizing that a girl this good-looking with moral indignation who can make a good joke about a wax museum probably already has a boyfriend, probably a football player or a rodeo star.

"We'd better get started," I say

"What do we do?"

"I'll pick him up and put him in this chair and you strip the bed, all right?"

"OK."

"Then we'll change his sheets, close his eyes, put on his pjs, comb his hair, give him a shave –"

"Give him a shave?"

"Yeah." I push his arm down and it slowly rises back up. "A dead man can grow a fairly good beard in a few hours' time. We'll have to do something about these limbs too."

Norma blinks and swallows an apparent moment of revulsion.

I say, "Just throw all the linens in the corner. There's a bottle of disinfectant in the bathroom under the sink. Sing if you want. It helps."

"What would I sing?"

"Yo ho ho and a bottle of rum?"

"Can you open a window?"

"The place is climate-controlled. The windows don't open."

"Like a prison," she says.

"You're getting the idea."

I pluck Mr. Joliet off the bed. He is a gaunt little cadaver with a pencil mustache and a bug-eyed face that reminds me of the later, bitter years of Ty Cobb. I wield his icy bones to the chair. His upper lip clings dryly to the pink and swollen gum. He has a flat, grotesque, yellow pig's nose. His glassy eyeballs glare out at me with furious unforgiving. The individual strands of his sparse hair spike out of his cold, polished lemonade head as if someone has touched a live wire to the back of his neck.

Norma strips the bed and throws the fouled sheets into the corner. She moves in lunges and violent snatches, panting, wisps of damp hair falling over her face.

"So, where do you live?" I say, wiping the green muck off of Mr. Joliet's legs and backside.

"Mt. Helix."

Where the rich people live, I think. "You married?"

She laughs. "I was married when I was sixteen, then I got a divorce. You know, I have a daughter. I've been taking care of her."

"So you live with your folks?"

"Yeah. How do you tuck the sheets in? I don't know how to make a hospital bed."

"It isn't important," I say, pulling his arm down and letting it snap back up like a slot machine handle. "As long as it's tucked in."

"This has got to be the weirdest day of my life," she says.

I swing Mr. Joliet up onto his fresh sheets. The fluid settles in his lungs with a sound like wet gravel turning in a cement mixer. The eyes will not stay closed under the pressure of my fingertips. I shove his knee down and watch it creep back up.

"I've got to go to the med room," I say. "Get some restraints and some weights for his eyes. Will you be all right alone with him?"

"I need some air," she says. "I'll wait for you outside."

When we return to the room a few minutes later, Mr. Joliet has found his original position. We wrestle him back down. Norma holds his arms while I crosstie them across his chest to the rails. The knee appears to be raised for all time, like the drum-major exhibit in the Museum of Modern Man. It takes all of our groaning combined weight and a great unsettling crunch to pop that knee flat. Then it slowly rises back. Norma covers her eyes. "It's like he's still *alive*."

One of the fishing weights slides off his face. An eye peels open. Then the heil-Hitler arm comes swinging out of its restraint and slaps me in the face.

"I'm going to quit," says Norma.

"I'm the one who just got slapped."

"I don't have to work," she says.

"Then why are you here?"

She takes a deep breath, staring at Mr. Joliet, and licks her dry lips. "I don't know. I thought I could help people."

I feel a sudden desperately strong attraction to her. I have just been partly responsible for the disappearance of an innocent woman unable to negotiate in society, and here is a man abandoned by his family who has been dead for more than four hours, and I am thinking about frolicking with the new aide, a single mother who has never had a job. Marry me, I want to say. Instead I say, "Can you sit on his chest?"

"What?"

"Just for a sec, till I tie him down…"

At last he is supine, a double top sheet stretched tautly across his mischievous limbs. We prop three pillows under his head. I gum his eyes shut with a dab of Poly-Grip on the lashes. We grease back his hair. Norma gives him a shave with his electric razor, missing a dime-size patch of bristle on his chin. Her hands are shaking. The knee is beginning to creep back up.

Hutchins pokes her redhead through the door. "Is he ready yet? His daughter is here…"

"Ready," I say, "as he'll ever be."

Hutchins strides into the room. "You've done some good work here," she says, hands folded behind her. "I want to thank you both. I know it was a difficult situation." She moves in closer, then stops all at once and appears to sink, as if she has just hit a bed of quicksand. "Better leave the lights off," she adds. "And spray some air freshener around. Cripes. And take that underwear off the lamp."

9.

I ACHE WITH THOUGHTS OF NORMA ALL NIGHT AND CATCH Frank Sinatra glimpses of her sublime form as she flails along with us through the senescent mists trying to manage 128 patients with only four aides. I feed the ancients, turn them, change them, scribble hasty notes that will never be read in their charts, dump their catheter bags, swap out their colostomy bags, check their blood pressure and sugar. It's like working in a giant orphanage after Nazis have killed all the nuns. The call lights blink off and on inanely down the halls. The patients howl and gurgle and moan. They heave their plastic water pitchers and copies of *Modern Maturity* overboard. Amy, the gorgeous but lackadaisical drug nurse, keeps reloading her med cart with Thorazine. The energetic and devoted Hutchins zigzags from room to room, chipping in with the menial work. I don't take a dinner break. I didn't bring dinner anyway. I am thankful to be busy. Eleven o'clock comes before I know it.

I wait exhausted by the time clock to say goodnight to Norma, trying not to think of Bev and pretending to be absorbed by a notice for physical therapy night classes at Grossmont Junior College on the bulletin board. Linda, mother of six, says goodnight. Horse comes in, refusing to meet my eyes. I can stare at her better this way. What conformation! What bodily gleam! What quivering flanks! Her stout, slow features, quick flare of nostrils, and scent of liniment and sweat excite me even more. When Norma finally enters the room I have to mentally slap myself in the face. Her hair is tied up, exposing her lovely neck. Color has returned to her cheeks. I drink her in like a bee drowning in a bottle of sarsaparilla. She can't figure out how to insert the card.

"How do you work this thing?"

"Just plunk it in," I say. "Like this. They pay you the same no matter what time you stamp on it. You're coming back tomorrow, aren't you?"

"Yeah," she says wearily. "I guess. I never dreamed when I got up this morning I'd be sitting on a dead man's chest singing yo-ho-ho and a bottle of rum."

I'm about to ask her out (really, I am) when Chula strides into the room and swats me on the behind. I've never appreciated how truly coarse she is until I see her standing next to Norma. Norma frowns. "Well, good night," she says, turning out of the room.

"It won't be this bad again," I call to her. "Today was kind of a freak. Mercury in retrograde. I'll see you tomorrow."

Chula grabs her card and slams in her time. "What crawled up your pants, *chilito*?"

"Nice girl, Norma," I say. "Did you meet her?"

"Yeah, kind of a fat ass, though, huh?"

"I didn't notice."

"Oh, you noticed. She doesn't have any tits either."

"I'll see you later, Chula."

"Hey…"

I hop in my car and drive straight over to Pat's, who lives only two blocks away. The door is locked. There is no answer. I have this feeling she is inside, drinking quietly. I stand there and listen. Because the walls are so thin I can't be sure if that's her stereo, turned down very low, or someone next door. A phone rings distortedly down the hall. I walk back down the stairs and tour the swimming pool area. It's late spring but still cool, the smell of honeysuckle and redwood bark and chlorine steam in the air. No one is out. The pool and sauna are closed. I stick my head in the party room, where Pat sometimes shoots pool, but it's empty. Some party room.

I drive to Diablo's, Pat's bar on El Cajon Boulevard, but her Malibu is nowhere about. Her car is not parked on Bev's street either. The windows of Bev's apartment are still dark. On the sidewalk out front, I kneel to have a second look at those footprints, but they are gone, whisked away by dog paws or landlubbers on polyethylene wheels or scrubbed clean by the skirts of lonesome ghosts returning home late to the graveyard. I find the door unlocked and the rooms just as we left them, Bev's drink still on the telephone table. The ladybugs in their multitudes shuffle silently on the walls. I feel suddenly pressed down by a great weight. The smell of raspberry tea and slowly decomposing wood makes me depressed. I pick up the phone and dial Pat's number. I let it ring fifteen times. I still have the feeling she is home.

I'm happy to find the beer in Bev's refrigerator. I open one and sit down in Bev's chair to think. The phone rings, startling me, then stops. I'm tempted to pick it up, but I don't want to spoil the caller's next attempt. I think it might be Bev, but then I wonder: *why would she be calling her own house?* The pines begin to rustle and swish outside and I can smell their green vanilla turpentine mixed with the crab leg and cigarette butt scent of the ocean only two miles away.

I should leave but I don't know where to go. I don't want to go home. I clean the place up a bit, remove the empty brandy bottle from William Holden's forehead, and take a tour of the apartment, half expecting to find Bev at every turn, altered, broken, expired in the horrible manner of Roger Joliet. I wonder if bums or derelicts or junkies have discovered a free flop and are waiting around the corner for me to leave, crouched next to a coil of sunflower-seed-studded human excrement with the terror of social oppression in their eyes. I turn on all the lights to scare them away. The cat startles me. I kneel to pet her but she darts back under Bev's bed.

On Bev's dresser is an old photograph of her and someone who looks a lot like her. I think it is probably her brother. I idly open a drawer and there, inside a white box stuffed with cotton, I find a glass syringe with a needle in it. Hospitals don't use glass syringes anymore. I wonder if Bev is a diabetic, or perhaps needs adrenaline for asthma. It could have been the brother's too. Pat has told me that he was in the armed services and died long ago, but Bev will not talk about him. In the photo brother and sister look so much alike they might be twins. Bev was not so ugly then, or at least some felicity or sense of the future seems to animate her much younger face. I imagine that the two came out here from the east together on a California Dream Adventure. She came to stay with him while he served his military term. When he died, she simply stayed, having nothing to return to.

The wind outside bumps along the windows. I call Bev's name softly. It seems as if she is here. It takes me a moment to get up the courage to look under the bed. I check the closets. On the nightstand on a Haldol-stamped memo pad is a note: *Dear Deborah, Something has happened. It's them again, them. I wish you were here. I am. I am...* The last word trails to a jagged line. I wonder who Deborah is. I fold the note and put it in my uniform pocket, where there are still cookie pieces from the night before. The phone rings twice, then stops. I return the notepad to the drawer and walk back down the hall into an empty living room. Unsettled, I turn on the radio. It takes a minute for the tubes to warm, and I wheel the big knob until I whistle in some Doris Day music way down at the end of the dial, something I imagine Bev would listen to while reading the illustrated biography of Jeanette MacDonald. I try to imagine for the millionth time what could've happened to her. I keep seeing her walking along railroad tracks, babbling and tipped over to the left like Helen the Answer Woman.

The cat meows at me. I don't know how long it's been since she's eaten. In the refrigerator I find a powdered lemon cake wrapped in foil and two chicken tacos in a white to-go bag. The cat says no to chicken tacos, even though I am considerate enough to remove the lettuce. I open another beer and begin to explore the kitchen cabinets. One cupboard is packed entirely with cans of cat food. Persia is staring at me petulantly from around the corner, still miffed about my chicken taco foray. I open a can of Salmon Savor Pussy Gourmet and scrape it into her empty plastic bowl. I change her water. She scampers huffily away down the hall. I say, "Here, kitty, kitty," but the cat is deaf and probably hates me for being responsible for the disappearance of her master.

Now someone is rapping on the screen door. It must be Pat, I think, the way she is knocking with such big-knuckled firmness. Who else would be here at this time of night? Not a vendor or a neighbor. I hurry out of the kitchen. I can only see an outline standing against the screen door. Way too narrow for Pat and slightly crouched, like an older person. I think for a moment it must be Bev. Something is wrong with her...

"Hello," I call cautiously from four feet away. "Who is it?"

"It's the landlord," comes the sharp reply. "Who are you?"

"I'm Edgar Donahoe," I pipe up bravely, moving in closer now. I can't see his face because of the streetlight behind him. "I'm a friend of Bev's."

"Is Bev here?"

"No. Not this minute."

"What are you doing here?" he demands.

"We work together at the hospital," I explain.

"Where is she?"

"She went out. She's with my friend Pat."

"Oh, yes, Pat, the big girl?" He seems to be shading his eyes with his hand. "The nurse?"

"Right. They should be back soon. They just went to the store."

He is nodding. He appears to be satisfied with my lie. I know it helps that I'm dressed all in white. "I'm glad to see that Bev has some friends," he says. "She spends too much time alone, bless her heart."

I try to smile. We have an awkward silence. I would invite him in, but it's not my house.

"For a minute there I thought you were breaking in," he says. "Hard to trust people anymore. Neighborhood's really gone to pot. When Bev first came here back in '57 this was one of the nicest areas in the city. She lived with her brother then."

"Yeah, I know."

He is shaking his head now. "Too bad, isn't it?"

I have to pretend that I know more about Bev than I do. "Heartbreaking," I say.

"She was more outgoing then, you know. They used to bowl, and they danced too. Ballroom. She was a fine dancer. They were close, maybe too close, small town kids never comfortable in the city… How long's that been now?" His hand moves to his chin. "Nineteen years?"

"Long time," I say.

"Now, what has she got? *Neighborhood Watch* signs, kids on dope, kids peddling dope, kids trying to steal your TV to pay for their dope. No wonder she doesn't go out…" He lets out a sigh.

"Do you want me to give her a message or anything?" I say.

"No, no. Just tell her Winston stopped by. She usually pays rent on the twenty-eighth."

"Oh. What day is it?"

"It's the twenty-eighth. I was by this afternoon, but she wasn't home. Funny, can't remember the last time she wasn't home at two in the afternoon. Creature of habit, you know, like her Mexican food and her Sunday bus rides downtown to pick up those used movie magazines. Well, not due till the first, anyway. Never late in nineteen years," he adds.

"She ought to be back any minute," I say. "You sure you don't want to come in and wait?"

"Well, no, already past my bedtime." He lifts a hand and it flops back to his side. "Just a little worried, that's all. Just tell her that Winston stopped by. I'll talk to her tomorrow. I know she'll be home in the afternoon. I don't bother her in the mornings. She likes her sleep. Just thought I might catch her after she got off work. She's a good tenant, that Bev. Good person. Heart of gold."

"She sure is," I say, with a grin a light breeze would shatter.

"Good night now, Edgar."

I watch him walk away down the flagstone steps. Then I call Pat's house again but there is no answer.

10.

ON SUNDAY, PAT CLOCKS IN FIVE MINUTES LATE AT THE HOSPI-tal. I've been lingering at the nurses' desk hoping to God she would show. I have not seen her since the fateful night, and I am frazzled from the burden of lying endlessly all by myself. I practically sprint to the clock room and steer her down a hallway out of earshot of the front desk, where I think we are being observed with suspicion. There is a good deal of murmuring at the hospital because Bev has not shown up for the third day in a row.

Pat is wearing a red nylon country-and-western nurse's aide uniform that distinguishes itself from a leisure suit by the name badge, "Pat Fillmore, Nurse's Aide," above her pocket. She is also wearing pink sneakers with red shoelaces. Her eyes match her uniform and she smells faintly of wine.

"Where have you *been*?" I say.

"Where do you *think*?" she hisses, swiping her hand through her hair. "I've been looking for BEV."

"Where?"

"EVERYwhere."

"You don't answer your phone. You don't answer your door. Why didn't you come get me or call me or something?"

"Because it's *my* fault."

"We're in this together."

She sticks an angry thumb into her chest. "It's MY fault."

"Her rent's due tomorrow."

"What?"

"Rent. You know, money you pay every thirty days to keep from getting wet?"

"How do you know?"

"I talked to the landlord."

"Today's Sunday," she says.

"Her rent's still due."

She licks her lips. "We'll pay for it."

"With what?"

She closes her eyes and her lips make a white scar as she pulls them against her teeth.

War Nurse appears at the end of the hall. War Nurse spells for Hutchins on the weekends. She is a wide, stoic woman, entirely gray except for the starched white uniform and dab of cap. She has served in three military campaigns and is accustomed to the action, adventure, and authority of the battlefield, not the dreary cold storage of the rest home. Any socializing outside the break room is perceived by her as lollygagging and punishable by fifty lashes. She flares her nostrils like a bull about to make a charge.

"Shit, I gotta go, Eg," says Pat. "I'll talk to you on break. Five."

The police arrive before that. We are summoned as a pair to the front desk. Every employee in the hospital except for Horse has assembled.

Jackie the Jesus Freak and Adrian De Persiis Vona, the weekend orderly, are seated at the circular nurse's desk with War Nurse and Amy the drug nurse. Chula is propped in the med room door making obscene gestures at me with fist and tongue. Norma Padgett, the new aide, stands off at a distance, queenly and sedate, arms folded across her chest. The *minute* all this trouble blows over I am going to ask her out.

The interview is short and humiliating. I think War Nurse is letting her employees stand around and watch us get grilled because it probably makes her sentimental about a court martial she once presided over in the Korean War. One police officer is tall and wears a red blazer and special FBI indoor sunglasses that by emanation of thermal waves can determine if someone is lying. I wonder if he can see the foil sheet of LSD in my wallet. I think if I go to jail I may never see the free world again. The other cop is squat-necked with a black mustache glued on straight out of the box. He wears a regular police uniform though he appears to be carrying extra walkie-talkies. I think these officers should at least have the consideration to take us outside and interview us privately.

Pat and I have not had a chance to coordinate our stories. Apparently a neighbor has been watching us closely and called the police, who seem to have a better idea of our comings and goings at Bev's apartment than we do. We are caught in several lies. Our fellow employees are regarding us with reproach. Our answers get briefer, more and more childlike and vague.

Thank goodness for Helen the Answer Woman, who keeps passing us as she makes her laps around the hospital and pausing for a moment to converse. "Oh, sure," she intones severely, her head tipped over as she stares at the officers. "Nanderndee-dee-furfle-dee-*furrr*."

Pat, who bristles easily under the prod of authority, finally blurts indignantly, "We haven't done anything *wrong*."

"No one said you did, Miss Fillmore," calmly replies the tall cop in the red blazer, who looks to me like a security guard at a golf tournament. "We're simply acting on a missing person's report. You were the last ones apparently to see her. If you can tell us what you *did* do."

"We played some cards," Pat replies sulkily. "Listened to the radio, and drank tea."

"And what time did you leave?"

"Uuuhm. What time was it, Edgar?"

"Late," I say. "I don't recall."

"How late? Four?"

"Yeah, probably."

"The neighbor said six."

"Could've been."

"And you continued to return that morning, till at least ten."

"We went to the store."

"A couple of times," I add.

"It was late," says Pat. "Or early, depending on how you look at it. Bev had a cold. We wanted to make sure she was OK."

"Were you drinking or using drugs at this party?"

"We were just drinking tea," says Pat. "Oh, and we had a little black-berry brandy, didn't we? Bev herself does not drink."

The cops nod doubtfully and stare at me. They don't stare at Pat. It is that special look of disgust people reserve exclusively for orderlies.

"Do you have any idea where she might be, Mr. Donahoe?"

"None whatsoever," I say.

"What about the neighbor?" says Pat. "She seems to know more about us than we do."

The tall cop shakes his head as if to say, this won't do.

"I called the police," Pat lies. "They said there wasn't anything they could do."

The officers bend their heads, scribble our names and numbers down, nod gravely, and take their leave.

At dinner break, darling dashing weekend orderly Adrian De Persiis Vona, smock flowing, stethoscope tilted jauntily, joins us at our table with a meatball sandwich. Pat is drinking coffee and eating Funyuns out of the bag. I am having tuna salad my mom packed for me and a half-pint of chocolate milk from the machine. Adrian has tightly curled, afro-sheen hair and a dimple in his chin that seems to need a Spanish peanut or a pearl glued into it. Normally he does not deign to eat with us, though he attends our parties sometimes if there is an aide on the program who interests him. He is sex-crazed, I believe, worse than me, a satyr of some kind. His blue eyes shine in his wide doll-like face as he takes a seat across from us and sets down his meatball sandwich, which is still wrapped tightly in steaming tissue paper.

"To what do we owe this great honor, Doctor Ravioli?" Pat greets dryly.

Adrian winks at me. "My curiosity is aroused," he says.

"Curiosity killed the cat."

"Satisfaction brought him back. What was with the cops?"

Pat's face is impassive. She sips from her coffee. "You heard. They were looking for Bev."

"Yes, I gathered, but why did they talk to you?"

Pat shrugs. "Because we're her friends."

Adrian examines the nail of his right index finger. "No, they talked to you because you saw her last."

"OK."

"And you didn't answer their questions."

"We answered all of them."

"The shut-in walks away into the night never to be seen again? I know Bev. I've been working here almost three years. You're not telling something."

"So, it's none of your business."

"You can confide in me," he says. "Tell Uncle Ade."

"Nothing happened."

"Your campaign is no secret, Pat."

"Well, at least I never tried to have sex with her on the floor in front of everyone," Pat snaps back.

Adrian has a history of public exhibition, and he, like most young people of my generation, appears to enjoy tallying his conquests, especially the exotic ones. His tally is much longer than mine. I was there at Pat's apartment the night he invited Bev for a romp on the carpet. Although everyone was shocked, and some I imagine even privately delighted, Bev simply asked to be driven home. She seemed more sad than embarrassed or upset. I thought she would never come to one of our parties again.

"Only nuns in this day and age want to die virgins," Adrian replies without a trace of humility. "And I have my doubts about that too. Every woman enjoys an occasional pass."

"Phhh," says Pat.

"I want to help," he says.

"Help what?"

"Help find Bev. She's my friend too."

"Adrian Cannelloni," Pat scoffs. "TV Detective."

"I've got resources you don't."

"Like what?"

"Like university and hospital access. Morgue records."

"She's not on a – goddamn it, Adrian."

"If she doesn't come to work for three days, doesn't answer her phone, and isn't sick in bed, she's either kidnapped, walking the streets, institutionalized somewhere, or dead. Bev doesn't walk out of her apartment at four in the morning unless someone physically *removes* her, so either you buffoons drove her somewhere and lost her, got her drunk and she fell through a sewer grate, or Captain Spaulding here gave her one of his magic tabs..." He raises his eyebrows at me as if he knows. I stonewall him and take a swallow from my empty chocolate milk carton. He opens his meatball sandwich. It looks like surgery to me, with the straight slit and the red mass of warm meat inside. He sprinkles cheese with a pinkie-extended flourish that reminds me he is first-generation Italian.

"You need to tell me what really happened," he says. "The more realistic we are, the better chance we have of finding her."

Pat heaves a sigh and glares. "Nothing happened."

"No, I don't believe that."

"What can we do?" she says. "I've looked EVERYwhere."

"I'll check hospital admission and morgue lists tomorrow morning," he says. "We'll start showing around and posting her photograph. We need a list of her relatives."

"There aren't any."

"You sure?"

"I'm sure."

Adrian has still not taken a bite of his meatball sandwich. "That's a pity," he says.

"The police are looking for her," Pat says.

"The police don't care about Bev," he says.

11.

I'M IN MRS. TOBBLEHOUSE'S ROOM A WEEK LATER WATCHING her brand-new Hitachi television set that her granddaughter bought for her. What a sharp picture. I think I might buy one of these when I get my own apartment. I change the channel, looking for a baseball game. Behind me comes a hideous deep-sea gurgling sound, and when I turn around Mrs. Tobblehouse has a giant red bubble swelling between her lips as if she is a bubblegum champ going for the record. Then the bubble snaps and blood slushes down the sides of her neck.

Mrs. Tobblehouse is a huge woman, all fat, with a terrace of five chins dripping a slick red as if she has been too heartily once again into the raspberry cheesecake. There is no doubt in my mind that she is completely deceased. Her head, however, is propped on the pillow in a way that makes her appear as if she is still watching TV. I am frozen for a moment. I have seen many dead people but never seen one actually die before. To feel her carotid artery for a pulse I have to press against her bloody throat. I don't find any pulse. Amy, the drug nurse, sticks her gorgeous head in the door.

"Edgar," she says. "We're going to have a séance tonight."

I look up. "What?"

"A séance," she says. "Is there anything wrong?"

"She just died," I say.

"Who?"

"Mrs. Tobblehouse."

"What happened?"

"I was watching her TV and she just snorkeled up this big bubble of blood."

Amy plunges into the room. Fresh out of vocational school, she is not the brightest nurse who ever lived. What she lacks in brains, however, she makes up for in looks, even if her cougar green eyes are set a bit too closely together. I know her brother from high school. Her boyfriend is a twenty-two-year-old college track star with arteriosclerosis, which Amy explains with a perfectly straight face by saying that he is a Virgo.

"GI bleed!" she cries. "She's hemorrhaging! Call a code! I'll start CPR. Call a code, will you?"

"She's dead," I say.

"Well do something, can't you?"

"Like what?"

We stand over the corpse. Mrs. Tobblehouse stares at the television, baby blue eyes scumbled over with clouds. Amy is still holding Mrs. Tobblehouse's medication, a green and a white pill in a little paper cup. "I have to wash my hands," I say.

Amy is still staring at Mrs. Tobblehouse when I come out of the bathroom. Drug nurse, in my opinion, is the cake job of the whole place. Amy doesn't touch or clean patients, dress wounds, pour peroxide down decubitus caverns, mop barf, lay bedpans, mine for fecal impactions, insert catheters or nasal gastric tubes, prepare corpses, or tackle organic psychotics; she just drives around her plastic compartmentalized drug truck all night in the twilight of desire, handing out dreams, last call for Nembutal. If she's so inclined, she can help herself to any of the more select medicines, synthetic opiates, pharmaceutical cocaine. Around her pretty tanned neck she wears a necklace of puka shells, and I lust for her vaguely in this room full of corpulent death. "How horrible," she says.

"Terrible," I agree.

"I'll go tell Hutchins," she says.

I glance back at the Hitachi. "Whose house is the séance at?"

"Who? Oh, mine. I just got a Ouija board. Hutchins is going to show me how to use it."

"Can I invite Norma?"

"Sure," she says. "The more the merrier."

I find Norma pouring whipped peas down a plastic tube into the nose of Mr. Zanduchi. I haven't been able to talk to her decently with all the recent commotion surrounding Bev and the generally perceived opinion that because I am having an affair with Chula and am somehow responsible for the disappearance of Bev, I am a cad.

"Little late for dinner, isn't it?"

"Hutchins just put the tube in him. He hasn't eaten in two days."

Mr. Zanduchi, a stroke patient, is gulping and gagging, his hands grabbing through the air. I doubt if he has ever eaten before without the aid of hands or mouth. Actually, he has decided to quit eating, hence the tube. He does not want to live anymore, but there will be none of that here under the auspices of science. He clutches and gags. He is dining out of thin air, unable to taste his food, with only the sensation of a plastic tube stuck in his throat.

"Do you want to go to a séance?" I say.

"A séance?" she says, tilting her plastic funnel of peas for a better drain. "Where?"

"At Amy's house."

"I've never been to a séance before," she says.

"Me neither."

"Who are they contacting? Anyone I know?"

"I didn't ask."

"Maybe your friend, Bev."

"No," I say. "Bev's not…"

"Not what?"

Amy lives in Kensington on the second floor of a small redwood-shingled apartment complex that juts out over the brushy lip of a canyon, just waiting for an earthquake. The Ouija board sits on the kitchen table. Chula and Jackie the Jesus Freak and Hutchins are sitting around it. Pat and I have come together in separate cars. Norma rode with me. I pretend that she is my girlfriend, soliciting to her and moving my hand around the back of her waist without actually making contact. Chula scowls at me. At the counter in the kitchen Amy is breaking ice cubes into a bucket.

Pat has never seen a Ouija board before. "What's this thing?" she says, indicating the pointing device.

"That's the planchette," says Hutchins, who has changed into some kind of East Indian costume, including a gypsy-green half-moon scarf knotted complicatedly around her forehead.

Adrian appears at the head of the hall. "Can I be the little dog?"

"Where did he come from?" says Pat.

"I never miss a séance," says Adrian. "Well, well, if it isn't Norma, the Greta Garbo of Lemon Acres." He tips an imaginary cap. "How lucky can a man be, among the company of such beautiful ladies?"

"Can it, Ravioli," says Pat.

"I like my women like I like my ravioli," Adrian returns. "Plump and saucy and sitting on my tongue."

"This is a séance, Adrian," says Hutchins. "Not an orgy."

"You can't fault a man for optimism," he replies, clasping palms together at ear level like a heavyweight boxer in the bask of applause.

"You got anything to drink, Amy?" says Pat.

"We can't drink."

"What?!"

"Not until after we do the board."

"We must have clear perceptions," Hutchins elaborates. "Clear intentions."

"Oh."

"After we're through, we can," says Amy. "I've got some sloe gin."

"All right," says Pat, washing her hands in the air. "Let's get started."

"Who are we looking for?" I say.

"Bev, you turkey," says Jackie, who was a Zen Buddhist, a Vedanta Hindu, a Yogananda's Self Realization Church member, a White Chapel Acolyte, a Scientologist, a Divine Light Missionary, and a speed freak before she found Jesus. I think it was the speed that really helped her find Jesus. It must have been God Speed. She has done so much speed her teeth are black and her hair is fried on the top of her head in a crisp bun the color of a Brillo pad.

"Why are we looking for Bev through a Ouija board?" I say.

"Because the police are a bunch of boobs," says Pat.

"The boy's right," says Adrian. "If she answers, doesn't it mean she's dead?"

"Shut up, Adrian."

"Am I right or not, Hutchins?" he insists. "Is this a medium for communicating with the dead, or isn't it?"

"No, no, dummy," admonishes Amy. "We are communicating with the spirits. The ones above and below who know what we cannot know."

"Just sit down, Adrian, for Christ sakes," says Pat.

"I'm not putting my hands on it."

"Good, and keep your trap shut while you're at it."

"Hit the lights someone…"

Dark, the room suddenly smells of jasmine and sandalwood, as if a gang of new-age grannies has sneaked in from the parlor. The canyon light seeping through the louvered windows is blue. A flame waggles deep inside a single candle on the bookcase by the stereo under a black-light poster of Jimi Hendrix. With our hands piled on top of the planchette, Hutchins begins in a low bewitching tone to summon the spirits from beyond. I can't tell if the planchette is moving on its own, directed by an emanated ectoplasmic force, or if we are somehow manipulating the answers ourselves, but it whips around the board, answering test questions with alacrity.

"Who am I?"

H-U-T-C-H.

"What day is it?"

F-R-Y-D-A-Y (close enough).

"Do you know Beverley Fey?"

YES.

"Is she alive?"

YES.

(Sigh of relief from Pat.)

"Is she safe?"

YES.

(Another sigh from Pat.)

"Can you tell us where she is?"

The planchette swings suddenly downward, attracted to numbers: 1-1-1-4-9-3-5-1-8.

"It's a PHONE number!" cries Jackie.

"It's nine numbers," says Amy.

"Copy it down someone."

"I'll remember it," says Adrian.

"Can you please tell us the whereabouts of Bev?" Hutchins enunciates. What we spell is a mystery to everyone: D-O-N-T-O-N.

"Maybe it's two words," offers Jackie. "Like a name of a guy. Don Ton."

"Maybe you misspelled 'donut,'" says Adrian. "Or maybe it's wonton," he adds. "Maybe she's being held captive in a Chinese restaurant."

"That isn't funny, Adrian," Hutchins warns.

"No disrespect to Bev," he says. "She was a better aide than all of you put together. But do you really think you're going to find her through a game by Milton Bradley?"

"It isn't a game, Adrian," says Hutchins.

"Shut up, everyone," snaps Pat. "We're gonna lose contact…"

"Don Ton is the name of the guy who *kidnapped* her," pipes Chula.

"Or a man who knows where she is," adds Jackie.

"Or the name of the place where she is."

"Or the name of a *street*. It's an address."

"There aren't any nine digit addresses in San Diego," says Jackie.

"How do you know?"

"Because I delivered telephone books last summer."

"Stop it–" shouts Pat.

A clattering to our left startles us all, a scratching on wood, and then a door down the hall bangs open. A toy poodle, blue in the canyon light, bounds into the room. Amy stands to turn on the light. "Puddles," she scolds. "How did you get out?"

"Puddles the poodle," says Adrian with a grin. He is staring at Norma. I know this because I am too. She is sandwiched by admiration. She has not said a word since we arrived, not gossiped, not tried to cheapen or hog the ceremony. I am more impressed with her each time I see her, so quiet and noble and aloof. If I don't make some kind of claim on her, Adrian is going to steal her out from under me. He has already done this about seven times. I don't know what I have to offer her that Adrian can't do better.

"Who let Puddles out?" says Amy. "The door was locked."

"Ooh," says Adrian. "Maybe it was 1-1-1-4-9-3-5-1-8."

"Come on," groans Pat. "Knock it off. Throw that dog out and turn off the lights."

"Too late," says Hutchins.

"Why?"

"Look."

"What?"

The planchette is resting on the words at the bottom of the board: GOOD BYE.

Jackie lets out a gasp. She looks as if she has just seen a ghost, although she always looks this way.

"We broke it," Hutchins says.

"Broke what?" says Pat.

"The spell."

"Puddles broke the spell."

"Put your hand on the whadyacallit," Pat cries. "We've got to find out. Damn it, Puddles. Come on everyone."

"Next week," says Hutchins gently. "We'll try it again next week."

"Don Ton." Pat shakes her head miserably. Puddles begins to hump her leg. She shakes him off. "I don't like dogs," she says.

"They certainly seem to like you."

"Oh, I forgot to ask about *Bob*," blurts Amy. Bob is her track star boyfriend with the hardened arteries.

"Next week," says Hutchins, taking off her scarf.

"Drinks," says Pat, lighting a cigarette.

Adrian makes a disgusted face, waving at the smoke.

"You don't belong here, Dr. Science," says Pat. "You've got negative vibes."

"I believe in all kinds of supernatural phenomena," he answers.

"Yeah, like what?"

"Like the Oracle at Delphi. You know that the Oracle at Delphi was a simple girl raised in seclusion? She had no education but she predicted that Alexander would conquer the world, that Athens would fall to Sparta."

Pat grabs the planchette and spells out W-H-O C-A-R-E-S?

Amy twists open the bottle of sloe gin, fills plastic tumblers with

Seven-Up and ice, and begins to distribute the drinks. "You believe in ESP, Adrian?" she says.

"You mean eczema, seborrhea, and psoriasis?"

"These taste like Shirley Temples," says Chula.

"Doesn't this conflict with your faith, Jackie?" says Adrian.

"What do you mean? Sloe gin?"

"No. Sortilege. The occult. Whoring after wizards."

"Let's go get some pizza," says Pat.

"I'm up," says Chula.

"Me too," says Jackie.

"You up, Norma?" says Pat.

"Sure," she says.

"I gotta go," says Adrian. "I got a chem exam in the morning. Can I give you a lift home, Norma?" His eyes have that hypnotic look that you'll notice on boa constrictors just before they engulf a live piglet.

Norma stares up at him, entranced. "No," she says at last. "Thanks. I said I'd go with them for pizza."

"Suit yourself," he says, as if she has just denied the one and only great opportunity of her life.

The phone rings. "It's for you, Chula," says Amy.

"How does he know I'm *here*?"

"He probably called every number in the phone book."

"Tell him I went bowling."

"Take the phone, will you? I'm not lying for you."

Chula flounces up. She is back in a minute. "I gotta go," she says. "Big Chief Spark Plug is on the warpath. Edgar, can you give me a ride back to my car at the hospital?"

I glance around the table for help. I look at Norma last. Now, I imagine she will go home with Adrian and I will never have another chance with her.

12.

NO MONKEY BUSINESS, I VOW, DRIVING FAST TO GET CHULA home and hurry back to Norma and the pizza party before the Vultures of De Persiis Vona descend for the feed. Chula doesn't sit close to me, *como normal*. Maybe she knows that it's over between us. A woman has an instinct about these things. Now, however, before we're even out of Kensington, she has unzipped my trousers and pounced face first into my lap. One drink goes straight to her head, or maybe it goes to mine. I try to adjust my mirror so I can watch, but her ratty hairdo going up and down is all I can see.

I pull off along the side of the road, next to a small park, the blur of trees and the coals of juvenile delinquent cigarettes moving around a picnic table at the opposite end of the grounds. In a moment the seat vinyl is crunching under us and Chula is moaning in housewifely ecstasy. I check my watch and calculate arrival time: five minutes to finish here, five minutes to drop her off, maybe twelve minutes to get to Shakey's Pizza. I hope they wait. I hope they save me a beer. The rear window blazes suddenly with headlights. At first I think it is a cop. I note that I am parked on a dead end. The symbolism is not lost on me. *This was going to be the last time*, I think. *Fate must understand this.*

The door of the car behind me slams shut like the sound of a beer can getting crunched by a fifteen-pound mallet. Chula's body jerks under me. I try to bounce up to put on my pants, but my foot gets stuck in the steering wheel. Over the top of the seat all I can see against the glaring wall of headlights is a massive black shape moving toward me, its arms bowed like an ape's.

Chula grabs her blouse from the floor and presses it against her throat. "It's Mike," she croaks in terror.

Mike La Rue pulls open my door. He's short and compact as a barrel, bald as the North Pole, and somewhere in his early thirties. "Get out of the car," he says.

"I can't," I peep. "My foot is stuck in the steering wheel."

He laughs and reaches in to try to tear off my ear. Now he's on the other side of the car, jerking open the passenger door. He grabs his wife by the hair and yanks her down onto the dirt. Chula hits the ground with a thump and a shriek and he drags her away caveman-style.

I free my foot finally, pull on my trousers, and look back. Chula is sitting on the passenger side under the dome light. She is nude except for the blouse in her left hand clutched in some vestige of modesty. Mike slaps her face, growling all the while like a wild dog with its snout in warm intestines. She shouts the word "no" over and over as he slaps her tear-wet cheeks. I figure he must have followed us from the hospital to the séance and called from a pay phone.

I can find only one shoe. My chicken heart hammers alternately left, then right. Chula's clothes are scattered everywhere. I wonder what to do with them. Mike continues to slap his wife with the steady and dedicated conviction of a lumberjack. I can see the delinquents at the other side of the park, standing stock-still, memorizing the scene so they can describe it to the news team on Channel Eight. I decide to hightail it out of here, deal with the consequences later. I gather up her clothes and roll the panties like a pastry filling in the middle. I reach to turn the key. Mike is standing at my window again, puffed up like an angry lizard.

"Get out of the car," he says.

"Why?" I say.

"Get out of the car like a man. I'm going to kick the shit out of you."

What kind of man would get out of the car to have the shit kicked out of him? I hand him the pile of Chula's clothes as a peace offering.

He flings them to the ground. "Get out."

"No."

"Fine," he says. "I know where you live. I was in Nam, you know. I used to snuff those little fuckers in their huts."

"I apologize," I say. "I was wrong."

"Little late for that," he says, with a laugh and a sudden violent spasm of the chin. "You're a dead man."

I stare at my knees, my face hot with the illness of regret.

I hear him stomp away. His car door slams hard enough to break out the window. Then he guns the engine and fishtails out of the grass. As he passes, Chula looks over at me, still naked, her teary eyes black as spiders from running mascara. She can't see me very well, I don't think, because her glasses are still up on my dash.

13.

BECAUSE MIKE KNOWS WHERE I LIVE AND PAT AND I ARE PAYING rent (out of my Australia fund and her government checks) on Bev's apartment, I have a son-to-father talk with Landlord Winston the next morning. We are standing by his Chrysler New Yorker in blossoms of June sunlight spangling down through the pepper tree out on the curb in front of Bev's apartment. I've got Bev's mail in my hand, a Publisher's Clearinghouse Sweepstakes announcement, an electricity bill, and a needlecraft magazine promising thirty percent off all stock. I whack the bundle across my hip. "I want to move into Bev's apartment, Winston," I tell him.

Lord Winston, upset about Bev, has organized a neighborhood search effort that unfortunately has not yielded much, thanks in large part to general urban apathy and our attempts to conceal the facts in the case. "I don't like it," he grunts. He reminds me with his slicked down hair, plaid shirt, and colorful suspenders of an accordion player in a Greek polka band. "It's disrespectful to Bev."

"What if she calls or comes back in the middle of the night?" I say. "We've got to feed that cat every day too. You can't leave the front door open."

"No, you have a point there." He cradles his chin. "Tell me something, though, how come you told me that first night that Bev went to the store with your friend? You knew she was gone."

"I didn't want to alarm anyone. We were certain she would be back."

He levels a doubtful eye on me.

"Bev is my friend," I tell him. "Why would I plot to harm her?"

He considers this. Then he says, "Where do you think she went?"

"If I knew that I'd be there now. Pat and I have covered this town from pie shop to public restroom. We even waited for her six hours at her grocery store."

"The Lucky?"

"No, the Food Basket."

"Dad hang it," he blurts, flinging his hand out recklessly. "I'm fed up with these police. They'll give you a speeding ticket before you get your car out of the garage, but when your neighbor disappears there isn't hide nor hair of them. Want something done right gotta do it yourself, I guess.

Tell you what, I'll give you fifty off a month. And no security. Promise me one thing."

"What is it?"

"No parties. I know you're a good kid," he says. "But I was eighteen once too."

"Deal," I say, shaking his hand.

My mother, a gentle woman with washed-out gray eyes who attends court-reporting classes in the evening, is more difficult to persuade. I have to tell her the story of Bev with the particulars even more drastically modified to protect the fools responsible. I emphasize Bev's affection for screen stars and suggest that she may have gotten in trouble downtown as she made her weekly rounds buying used show business magazines. My mother's sympathies are easily aroused, and I don't feel good manipulating them. "Have the police been notified?" she says.

"Oh, of course, yes."

"Oh, that's awful," she says, pressing index finger to lips. "The poor woman. Why is it that the good people always get hurt?"

"I don't think she's hurt, Mom…"

"You know, this city is beginning to scare me, Edgar. It's getting so big. Do you remember when Lake Murray Boulevard used to be just one lane and there was nothing on the other side?"

"I remember," I said. "I used to go over and talk to the cows."

"Well," she says, "I think it's kind of strange living in someone else's apartment, but of course you're old enough to make your own decisions." She squeezes the sides of her glasses with middle finger and thumb, a gesture that tells me she is not at all comfortable with my decision.

"It has to be a secret, though, Mom," I add, trying not to fidget. "You can't tell anyone. I've made an arrangement with the landlord."

She stares at me, nonplussed.

"You can tell Dad, of course," I amend hastily.

"If you think it's a good idea, Edgar," she says. "Now, if you're in trouble, you know, that's why we're here…"

"Oh, no, *no*, Mom. Everything is *fine*. Don't you worry about *me*."

She smiles thinly. This is a woman so patient she has struck me only once in my life, the time I stomped on her periwinkles.

I move into Bev's place the following night. Pat is thrilled by my good sense. Now she doesn't have to drive over every morning to pick up the newspaper and the mail and go inside an apartment that she knows will be empty. It is Saturday, a mutual night off. We have gone to see a Society Is Hopelessly Corrupt double feature (I thought *Serpico* was innocently cynical, didn't you?) and stopped for two drinks at her saloon, where the leathery old divorced women at the bar fawned over me and the brawny young biker girls back by the pool table dreamed of throwing me through a window, while Pat introduced me all around the whole time, beaming and announcing cheerfully: "He's a surfer," or, "He works with me at the hospital," or "He's going to be a *doctor.*"

On the way back to Bev's apartment we buy two six-packs of Mickey's Big Mouth Malt Liquor in the wide-mouth green jars with the aluminum pull-tops that are ideal for cutting your wrists.

We sit in the stately living room under traditional electric dusk, sipping from our jars. I can feel time moving, even with the curtains closed. There are more ladybugs than ever. They like high corners and lampshades best. The ceiling hisses with invisible nests. How they continue to reproduce without gentleman bugs, I can't say.

"Your parents must be the coolest people on earth," Pat says. "To give you so much freedom. My mother, I had to fistfight her every time I wanted to go down to the rink."

"If my father knew what I was doing," I say, "he would probably hit me over the head with a shovel and bury me in the backyard under the lemon tree."

"At least you have a father."

Two ladybugs are crawling on my arm, one across my knee. "My father may not have a son soon the way I'm going."

"I won't tell anyone you're living here," she says. "I had a feeling that was going to happen. You know Chula's old man has been at the hospital every night the last three nights? Mike was in the Green Berets, you know. I think he served with John Wayne. Do you want another beer?"

"Do the Green Berets shit in the jungle?"

"Just remember what Winston said," she advises, returning from the kitchen and handing me a fresh jar of malt liquor. "No parties."

"And the Lord said: 'There shall be no parties.'"

"This isn't a party, is it?"

"Two people is not a party," I say. "Anyway, he meant don't tear things up, burn the furniture, or play music so loud the neighbors can't sleep. That's all he meant."

"That Winston is something else, isn't he? You'd think he was her dad the way he acts, over here twice a day all the way from Serra Mesa."

"Actually, he's her legal whadyacallit."

"Do you think he looks like Clarence on *Hee-Haw?*"

"No, more like Mr. Haney on *Green Acres.*" I stare into the green depth of my malt liquor. "Maybe we should just tell everyone the *truth*, Pat."

"Yeah," she says, "and lose our jobs and get thrown in prison and be outcasts of society for the rest of our lives." She tips up the brim of her straw hat with a thumb. "Why don't you turn on some music?"

I heat up the old radio, wheeling the great knob until I reel in some country and western.

Pat taps her foot to Bob Wills. "What do you think about the new aide?" she says.

"She's all right."

"I can't believe they replaced Bev already."

"What are they supposed to do? She's been gone almost two weeks."

"What kind of loyalty is that?"

"Loyalty?" I say. "Lemon Acres?"

"Yeah, but Bev's worked there twenty *years*."

"It's a disposable society," I say.

"Yeah," she says, flicking her Bic lighter. "Hey, you know who likes you, surfer boy?"

"Who?"

"Guess."

"Who?"

"Guess."

"I give up. Who?"

"You gotta guess."

"Lyndon Baines Johnson."

"No. Norma."

"Norma?"

"She told me at Shakey's last night."

"What'd she say?"

"She said she liked you."

"What does that mean?"

"It means she's got a crush on your skinny coffee-drinking butt. You oughta ask her out. Her parents are *rich*."

"So?"

"So, you could marry her and retire."

I get up and swing the dial until I find some oldies. *Do you love me, do you…?* "Why would I want to do that?"

"She doesn't act rich, though," Pat continues. "She wants to do it all on her own. She's got her feet right down on the ground. I like her. That girl has had a tough road to hoe."

"Row."

"What?"

"It's *row* to hoe. You don't hoe a *road*. Why would you hoe a road?"

"Hell if I know. All I know is that you should ask her out before Doctor Lasagna does. He's been slinking around her. He came back last night to Shakey's and stared at her like the rest of us weren't even there. You talk about a disposable society. He'll ruin her, you know that. This is a *real* girl, Eg, not a cheesy Mexican takeout dinner. You should ask her out."

"Maybe I will."

Pat heaves a heavy sigh and swirls her nearly finished jar of malt liquor. "Some people have all the luck," she mutters. "Do you want another one?"

I get up to look out the window, expecting to see Mike's car parked out front. I think about Norma and my wonderful luck, all overshadowed by a disturbed Green Beret and the karma of my cheap desire. Pat returns from the kitchen with fresh green jars. She has peeled off the tops, God bless her. Opening a jar of Mickey's is like opening a can of sardines. You have to have strong wrists and be careful not to slash a vein right at the end there when the tail of that razor lid finally swings loose. "Where you gonna sleep," she says, "on her bed?"

"No, no. On the couch."

"It's a nice couch." She looks all around. She seems suddenly small in the grand room decorated with tarnished deer paintings and shiny red insects. "Cozy little place," she says.

"Yeah," I say. "All it needs is a 'Mortuary' sign out front…"

Pat lights a Marlboro 100 with her disposable Bic and props a foot up on knee. "What's his name, Doctor Linguini, called me this morning and said there were two Jane Does on a postmortem list at UCSD that fit the description of Bev. He said that one of them was a junkie, but he didn't see the other one. I didn't know what he was talking about. What's a postmortem anyway?"

"An autopsy."

"An *autopsy*?" she says. "I thought it was a breakfast cereal."

I take a good long haul from my jar.

"Other than that," she adds quietly. "Nothing."

"No news is good news."

"It's better than bad news." She blows smoke out her nose and glances up into the darkness of the ceiling. "I wish we had good news."

"It hasn't even been two weeks." A ladybug put-puts past my nose, its wings a blur.

Pat finishes half her beer in one tilt. The phone begins to ring, then stops. She looks over at it, then at me.

I sing along with the Beach Boys on the radio: … *and she'll have fun fun fun till her daddy takes her T-shirt away…*

"Do you have plenty of cat food?" says Pat, arching her eyebrows at me.

"If you're hungry I can scramble you some eggs."

"Har-dee-har."

"Where is that stupid cat anyway?" I say.

"Here, kitty kitty," she says.

"The cat is deaf."

"Well I don't know sign language."

The cat peeks at us from around the corner.

"It's OK, kitty kitty," I say.

"Now, who's talking to the cat?"

Pat leaves the minute the Mickey's are gone, about one o'clock that morning. I walk her to the car. Maybe if Mike is lurking somewhere down the block, observing me, or perhaps has climbed a tree, or rented the apartment across the street in the pursuit of his joy of hunting the Slender-Horned Adulterer, he will see what a bruiser I hang out with and have second thoughts about an attempt on my life. The moon through the trees is a dirty chocolate color and loaded with toffee chips. It is a cool night this close to the coast, the smell of salted kelp on the breeze. Pat wallops me on the back. I check with my tongue to see if I still have all my fillings. I can see that she is miserable. She climbs into her Chevy Malibu with the turquoise-blue vinyl top, and I watch her squeal away around the corner.

PART III **Beauty Is in the Eyes of William Holden**

14.

is still checking with me twice daily for developments on his tenant of
nineteen years. I also believe he wants to make sure I don't burn her apartment down. Tonight I have just gotten off work and I am watching the
Tonight Show with Johnny Carson, eager to see Charlie Callus, one of my
favorite comedians.

Winston knocks on the door in the middle of the monologue. *"What's
all this fuss about plutonium? How could something named after a Disney character be dangerous?"*

"Hello, Winston," I say, buttoning my shirt. "Come in." The TV laughs
behind me. I have two beers in the fridge but I won't open one until he
leaves. Johnny tugs at the knot on his tie and says: *"The difference between
divorce and legal separation is that a legal separation gives a husband time to hide
his money…"* Three large greenish moths have flattened themselves onto
the screen to absorb the laughter drifting all the way down from Burbank.

"Any word?" says Winston, deadpan, looking around the room.

"No," I say. "Sit down."

Winston never sits. He won't stay long. I'll give him my no-news. He'll
give me his. He'll wring his hands, glance around at the ladybugs, patrol
one of the two yards, wash up in the bathroom sink, shake his head, then
leave. He is wearing lime-green suspenders and snaps them nervously over
his plaid shirt as he paces back and forth, the phantasmic gray light of the
television flickering over his trouser legs. *"I know a man who gave up smoking,
drinking, sex, and rich food. He was healthy right up to the day he killed himself…"*

"Nothing," I say. "I keep getting phone calls but they always stop mid-
ring."

"I get those too." He shoves his hands down into his pockets. "I think
it's the phone company."

I've been thinking lately it might be ghosts. I get at least one call per
night. It worries me that her brother might have been looking after her,
perhaps even talking to her, and now he is mad at me like the cat and
everyone else. I read recently in *Ellery Queen* that ghosts especially like the
telephone.

Johnny is swinging his golf club now, segueing with blare of brass and splatter of applause into the series of used car, laxative, and sleep-aid advertisements that make you wonder if you'll ever see Johnny's sympathetic Midwestern face again.

"I called the police again today," he says. "I was talking to the girl at the bureau desk there. Nice girl. You talked to her?"

"No, I haven't."

"She says there are something like half a million people who disappear every year. Thin air. Says most of them are trying to get away from their families, runaways and deadbeat fathers, that type of thing." He folds his arms tight and high across his chest.

"Not the case with Bev," I say.

He shrugs and claps his hands. "Who knows?"

"She doesn't have a family to get away from," I say.

He scratches his head as he stares at the floor. "Well, who's her family? Aren't *we* her family?"

My attention swings to Truman Capote as he sashays out onto the stage to rippling, bright, and titillated applause. He is wearing a cape and matching purple tam and appears to be drunk or high. I have never read anything by Truman Capote, even though he is famous. His gestures and voice are too squirmingly affected for me. I'm not much for murder books anyway. If I want to read about murder I'll open a newspaper.

Winston watches Truman without seeing him. Then he goes out through the kitchen door and pokes around outside. I don't know what he expects to find.

"I've got the worst feeling," he says, returning a few minutes later.

Charlie Callus is on now, honking, trumpeting, and blathering in his patented long-armed crouch. He isn't funny tonight. I stand up and turn off the television. "What is it?"

"I don't know." He looks left, swallows. "Gone almost a month now. Bad, bad." He smooths the hair along his temple with his pinkie. "I won't be by tomorrow. Wife and I are driving up to Temple City to visit her sister."

"All right."

"I wrote down the number." He hands me a scrap of paper. "Call me if anything happens. I'll be back in three days."

After Winston leaves, I sit for a long time in the dark with a beer and think. I wonder what Johnny Carson would do in my situation. I know he has endured a lot of personal tragedy in his life too. Finally, I snap on the lamp and pick up a *National Geographic* I brought home from Lemon Acres with a story in it about the Great Barrier Reef of Australia. The phone rings before I can read the first line. I snap it up out of the cradle and listen to the fading babble of accusatory voices before I offer a hello and finally hang up.

Curious about the brother, I begin to comb through some of Bev's closets. If the ghost is her brother I would like to at least know his name. In the bedroom closet I find a packet of corroded batteries, a cookie tin full of buttons, a green wool coat with a shopping list in the pocket, a Yahtzee game with filled score sheets (she must've played by herself), and a box full of letters. I select one of the top letters. I see that it's addressed to Deborah Kerr in Klosters, Switzerland. I see that all the letters are addressed to Deborah Kerr. This one is dated February 25, only three months ago. I begin to read, feeling wrong. The handwriting is neat and small.

Dear Deborah:

I turned thirty-seven yesterday. I don't care much for birthdays anymore. They come around so fast. My brother, Rodney, was a Christmas child like your Melanie, never extra presents. He always felt deprived. I feel old today, though I know I'm not. Melanie is twenty-eight now if I'm not mistaken. Of course you are right. There is more to life than having a family. Both Mr. Gabrielson in room 62 and Helen in 16 never had children either. I suppose as long as you can give your heart to something. I do love my patients, but they're gone so quickly. Everyone gone so quickly. In the last month two people from work have befriended me. They visit at the oddest times and whisk me away to parties. One is rough-cut with boots, a Barbara Stanwyck type. The other is a sunburned boy with wild hair. I don't know what he's talking about half the time. I don't mind them except for their drugs. I know they will tire of me soon. It was like that man I told you about ten years ago, who thought he would do me a favor by wooing me. I was glad when he returned to his wife. The pine trees out front have gotten enormous. I remember when I could look over their tops. Now they cover the entire house. I like their smell and the sound they make at night in the wind, though they are pushing up the sidewalk and Winston is talking about having them removed. Oh, my Lord, knocking. It's them again…

I let the letter fall to my side. I recall the disturbing note on the nightstand, *them again, them*. I see myself in Bev's eyes, an indecipherable sunburned boy with wild hair. I select another letter, reaching toward the bottom of the pile. This one is addressed to Pacific Palisades, California, and dated March 3, 1957:

Dear Deborah,

Rodney said he would take me to Grauman's tomorrow! We are so excited to visit Los Angeles and Hollywood. Rodney has two friends in Long Beach and we plan to have Mexican food along the harbor at a place he knows. As you know, we saw your beautiful home in Pacific Palisades above the ocean last summer. We are hoping there is some small chance we may see you, but don't worry. I know how important your privacy is. Me too! Rodney bought new brogues today and an atrocious tie. He says we're also going to Disneyland. I told him we won't have enough time! Please say hello to Melanie. I heard that you signed a three-picture deal. Congratulations. I must pack!

Your devoted friend,

Beverley Fey

The next letter in sequence is dated two months later. The paper is wrinkled and stained:

Dear Deborah,

I couldn't tell you until today. My brother rented a motorcycle with some friends and was killed in an accident on Midway Boulevard three days ago. I am still in a state of shock. They had the military funeral yesterday. The pain in my heart is unbearable. I am the only one left, Deborah. I wish I could've gone with him. Forgive me if I do not write again. Sincerely your friend…

No more correspondence for nearly a year, and then:

Dear Deborah,

It's been a lifetime, I know. But I've been with you every chance. I have learned to take satisfaction from work and from the hard work of others. I am also able to sleep again and the nightmares have almost stopped. I draw strength from your role in Heaven Knows, Mr. Allison. I feel as if I am living on an island, too, although no Robert Mitchum! I have always liked Robert Mitchum, even if he was in jail. I'm just happy you didn't marry him. I'm sorry to hear of your separation from Anthony. I know the pressures of Hollywood must be tremendous. I trust this letter finds you well…

I hear a rustling to my left. The lights dim for a moment. "Hello?" I say. Wind creaks through the pine trees. I fold the letters back up hastily and return them to their envelopes.

Bev's couch is plenty long and firm, but I still can't get comfortable on it. I cannot sleep in this house with the smell of her and the drums of Rodney's military funeral and the unmailed letters to Deborah Kerr. The ladybugs glitter and writhe palpably even in the dark. I stare up into the darkness and remember the first time I ever saw the Great Lakes. I was nine or ten years old. My uncle had a house on the beach on Lake Michigan. It was late summer, almost fall, but it seemed like winter. Bored with the adults and their bourbon and playing cards, I walked out to the beach by myself. I was an ocean boy. I had always loved the ocean and lived in it whenever I could, riding waves, black as a Senegalese. Lake Michigan looked like the ocean, except for the pitiful little curls of surf, worse even than Torrey Pines or North OB. It was a dark and drably greenish day, like a photograph taken from the mouth of a shipwreck's cave, and the beach was covered in ladybugs, every surface, every piece of driftwood and shrubbery and rock, every grain of sand. Even the water seemed to be clad in ungodly speckled insect sorcery. I stood out there in wonder at this strange dark Great Lakes day. Some of the ladybugs began to land on me. Do you know that ladybugs bite? I never suspected it. And I saw myself suddenly as a ladybug-covered statue, beaded and bloodless, my parents and uncle walking up and down the shore looking for me. *Where is that boy and where did all these ladybugs come from?* So I hurried back to the house in a terror, the little shiny bugs buzzing after me…

At three in the morning someone is knocking on the door. I think I am already awake but when I open my eyes I don't know where I am. This frightens me for a moment, and I remember Mike's promise to kill me. The knocking continues. Then again, it could be Bev, or maybe Pat stopping by on her way home from Diablo's. I have locked the door. I throw the blankets off my legs and swim across the room and open the door only a crack. Chula La Rue is standing on the doorstep.

"Let me in," she hisses. "It's cold out here."

"What are you doing here?" I say, scratching my head.

"I slipped out on him. He got drunk tonight. He's three shits to the ween."

I think I must still be dreaming. Chula does not appear to be humbled, disgraced, or chagrined by having the snot slapped out of her, but rather encouraged and even refreshed. How do I end up with these women? Daffy undesirable mothers-of-three mad with lust for teenage orderlies. I wonder if there is a slot for me on the *Phil Donahue Show*.

"Who told you I was here?"

"A little bird."

"Pat?"

"No, Jackie."

"How did Jackie find out?"

"What's the big secret? You holding Bev hostage or something?" She grips herself and shivers. "Lemme in, huh?"

"Weren't we almost murdered in a jealous rage a week ago?" I say. "Didn't your husband vow to kill me?"

"He's only talking. Let me in, come on."

"And now I find out he was a Green *Beret*? He's probably watching us through infrared binoculars from across the street."

"He's drunk, I told you. He won't find out, *piojin*. You think I'm going to tell him? You can't keep ignoring me. Are you going to let me in or not? It's cold out here, baby."

"No," I say.

"Why not?"

"I have a girlfriend now."

"Who?"

"Norma."

"*Chingado* – that fat-assed *perrita* with the buck teeth?"

I stare at Chula coldly, then slowly begin to close the door on her.

"Let me in!" she wails.

"Go away! We're through, Chula."

"Oh, no, no, you don't. Not that easy *ratoncito*. I drove all the way over here."

I've got my shoulder braced against the door and I speak through the last inch of gap. "Night, Chula."

"I'll tell him!" she shouts.

"Keep it down," I say. "The neighbors."

"Piss on the neighbors, *hijoles* – I'll shout if I want." She slams the screen door and stomps away down the flagstone walk swearing half in Spanish. She kicks my car door, denting it squarely and knocking off some more of my three-month-old Earl Scheib paint job. Then she turns and glares. I shut the door and throw the bolt. I hear her Dodge Dart roaring away so violently I wait for the sound of breaking glass.

15.

NORMA LAUGHS AT ME WHEN I ASK HER OUT FOR A DATE. WE ARE standing in room 112, Section C (or C Section as Pat likes to call it), with Mrs. Tucker, who spent her childhood on the Nebraska frontier and frequently hallucinates about Indians, and her roommate, Dotty, who repeats the phrase, "Shut up, Dotty," approximately one thousand times a day.

My confidence is shattered. "Why are you laughing?" I say.

"Because I was just going to ask *you* out."

"You were going to ask *me* out?"

Shut up, Dotty.

"Yes." Her large blue eyes glisten like wet sapphires. "Where were you going to say we should go?" I say.

"No, you first."

"How about the Charcoal House?"

"That's right down from where I *live*," she says.

"Have you been there before?"

"No, we always go to Anthony's or the Top Shelf."

"The Charcoal House is my favorite restaurant," I say. "The food is good, but the real reason I like it is they serve minors."

Shut up, Dotty.

"They do?"

"And how much money does the Alcoholic Beverage Commission have to send agents chasing after minors in little out-of-the-way restaurants? You drink, don't you?"

"Oh, yes. I'm a simple girl, raised in seclusion."

"Me too. Tomorrow then?"

"OK."

"I'll pick you up at your house at eleven minutes after seven."

"Seven eleven," she says.

Shut up, Dotty.

The secret to winning the confidence of a woman you like is getting her to drink wine. This is the only *concrete* thing I know at the age of eighteen, that and never have an affair with a crazy war veteran's wife. Norma is radiant in candlelight this evening. We have a table in the corner. I order chateaubriand for two, a carafe of house red, and punch in seventeen songs for a buck on the jukebox, including "Fire and Rain" twice.

I have become mature and suave after my second glass of wine. The burgundy spins in pleasant fumy volumes in the great caverns of my impressively empty adolescent skull. I feel benevolent and decide that I will marry Norma and become the father of her child. I think she is the type of woman who, despite her beauty, would agree to almost anything to escape her circumstances, living with her parents and stuck in a job at the bottom of the socioeconomic ladder, which makes us, glass number three, the ideal couple. This is the first time I have ever been out on a date with a woman I really care about. For the last ten minutes, she has been telling me in some detail about her daughter, Angie, who is three years old.

I try not to look bored. I don't mind children, but being so chronologically near to one myself perhaps limits some of my enthusiasm for them. I think about gesturing to the waiter for another carafe. There is a good feeling about this, the raising of the hand, the arrival of more warm grapy confidence.

Norma seems to sense my lapse in attention. "I'm telling you about this because when most guys find out I have a daughter they don't want to be with me anymore." Her eyes are already fuzzy from wine.

"I love kids," I say.

"I don't have a high school diploma either."

"I went to an experimental high school," I tell her, holding my glass aloft. "All they taught me there was the art of drug abuse and the glamour of being a social outlaw."

"You didn't go to the prom?"

"Did Clyde Barrow go to the prom?"

"I don't imagine he went to high school."

"There you go."

She stabs a piece of lettuce. "What is your point?"

"My point is that I don't know any more than someone who didn't go to high school."

"Yes, but you have your diploma."

"And I am working at a convalescent hospital."

"You're an intelligent person," she says. "You could go to college and become something."

"Yes, well, eventually I plan to."

"What would you like to be?"

What I would really like to be is in Australia, catching the reef curl as it glitters across the setting sun, but I can't say this. It doesn't sound responsible or ambitious enough, and I need to make a good impression not only because Norma and I seem perfect for each other, but also because I must maintain a social bulwark against the insane La Rue family, one or all of whose members may step through that door and kill me at any moment. So I say: "A doctor, I guess."

"You're as smart as Adrian," she says. "And you've got a much better personality."

"Personality won't be a problem for him," I say. "Because most of his patients will be unconscious anyway. He's going to be an orthopedic surgeon."

"What does orthopedic mean?"

"It's another word for millionaire. He won a full medical scholarship to Columbia University. He's actually quite a bit smarter than I am."

"What is he studying?"

"He's premed chemistry at UCSD. He's a straight-A student."

"How old is he?"

"Twenty-two."

"Oh," she says.

The chateaubriand arrives, flaming blue on its silver tray. The waiter carves off pink slabs and nods at us debonairly as he lays the meat across our plates. I finish another glass of wine and the room has deepened and mellowed to the color of love. Norma spears a morsel of tenderloin and turns it in the burgundy-colored light.

"You spend a lot of time with Pat."

"Yes," I say, "we're good friends."

"It's nothing more than that?"

I have to laugh. "No, we're just friends."

"Does she have anyone?"

"I've never asked. It's none of my business."

"Such a good person, though, so friendly, and always helping people." She takes a gulp of wine. "She's the one who told me to ask you out, do you believe that?"

"Yeah, matchmaking and astrology are her two favorite hobbies."

"She seems kind of jealous, though, don't you think?"

"Pat? Jealous? No. She's a full-blooded lesbian, you know."

"Yes, I've heard, from Montana."

"I said we might visit her tonight after dinner, if you're up for it."

"Sure."

"She'll be happy to see us, I think. She has lots of friends but she still gets the terrible lonesomes."

"That's all right by me," she says. "I know all about the terrible lonesomes. I told my mom I'd be home by midnight, though. She's taking care of Angie."

Perhaps I should not be driving. Certainly it is a mistake to visit Pat.

We knock and she greets us crouched at the door like Igor from the dungeon peering up at us from under the ledge of her furry brow, her hair like a shredded welcome mat, her face oily and flushed. Pat is plastered out of her mind, still wearing her red country-and-western nurse's aide uniform. She just got off work, how can anyone get this drunk in thirty minutes?

"Oh, it's the Eg and Normie Show," she slurs, straightening up slightly and weaving in the doorway. "Am I late?"

"Maybe we should go," says Norma.

"Fine, fine, just leave the ugly old mother bee alone," she says.

"No, that's all right," I say. "We'll come in for a minute."

"Oh, WHEEL come in for a minute," she mocks, her lips screwed back from her nubby teeth. "Isn't that a kindness to me? Spectrac – or however you say that. MOTHER bee? What the hell is that?" She seems to be falling backward in front of us as we enter the room but she manages to stay on her feet, muttering and jabbering deliriously the whole way: "I'm shickled titless. Wait a minute, what hap'med to my…I'm not only shickled, I'm TITless. I probably lost my fuzarus. Mim mim." She clears her throat and grapples with her larynx. "How was your DATE?" she says, her face suddenly composed, her hip thrusting spasmodically to the right. She has pedaled herself behind the kitchen counter in front of two bottles of Southern Comfort, one empty. She sets her hand on the out-thrust and spasmodic hip. "I hope you will enjoy me with a drink, a Comfy and orange perhaps or if you would prefer we also have orange and Southernnnn."

"I'll have an orange and Southern," Norma says, "Very light."

Pat stands at the counter weaving and staring at Norma as if she has never seen her before or possibly a pair of antlers is sprouting from her forebrain. Norma strolls around examining the Maxfield Parrishes. "Oh, this one's nice."

"I bought 'em in Tijuana," says Pat, pouring a good measure of orange juice all over the counter. "Tee FWA FWA. FWA FWA FWA. However the fugoosus you pronounce it. Here ya go, Normie," she says, "Light on the orange." The tall glass appears to be about seventy-five percent Southern Comfort.

"A little more orange for me," I say.

Pat whirls on me, her face cracked with rapt animation. "I heard a voice," she cries, finger in the air. "It said 'a little more orj for me.'"

"That was me."

"Son of a snuffgrinder. I thought it sounded famil-YER."

"We have to go pretty soon," I explain. "I don't want to get drunk."

"Oh, I didn't –Who got you drunk? Am I drunk? Boy," she says with a hot cackle, "I *feel* drunk."

"What time is it?"

Pat whips her wrist around and stares at no watch. "It's a monkey's ass in twenty-five freckles."

"We gotta go in thirty freckles."

"What? Sheezus. Gonna leave me all *alone?*"

"Norma has to be home by twelve, or she turns into a zucchini."

"Who turns into a zucchini?"

"Norma."

"Normie Norma, from California."

"And I'm going out in the morning," I say. "Early."

"Shiiiiit. You and that surfing."

Norma watches warily from the corner of the room. She sips from her drink and shivers. "Can I use your restroom?" she says.

"Where you going?" shouts Pat after her. "Don't you try to sneak out on me, Normabunny." Pat's attention returns to me. "Now that's a beautiful woman. You could haaaave her…" She flops her hand all around remonstratively as if she is slapping a misbehaved rabbit. "If you weren't going off all the time to that goddamn ocean *surfing.*" She spits the word out like a mouthful of tacks, wiping her mouth with the back of her wrist and draining half a glass of the orange-dampened liquor. "Well, now," she says, regarding the cocktail. "I wish we could smoke some mari-hoochie."

"I don't have any, Pat."

"I got some of these horseshit cigarettes when I was in Tijuana-TEEF-AWANAAA. FWA! FWA! With Carol Merrill Christmas Carol. What are horseshit cigarettes made out of anyway?"

"They're made out of horseshit."

"Really? You lying colostomy bag…" She lights one of the horseshit cigarettes, sucks in a long drag, and begins to cough. "This tastes like *horse-shit*," she cries, trotting to the balcony and flinging pack and lit dung over the rail. "Look out BELOW. Horseshit overboard! I love America," she mutters, returning to the room. "Gimme a cigarette, will you?"

Norma has returned, hair combed. She nods at me, ready to go.

"There she is," says Pat, her face suddenly glowing with pride and beatitude, her arms widening as if for an embrace. "I knew you wouldn't climb out the bathroom window. There isn't one anyway…" She mutters something insanely and incoherently off the side of her hand. "Norma's my beautiful buddy," she announces. "Beautiful buddies should always stick together, even if one of 'em is in love with somebody who will not be mentioned even though he happens to be right here in this room." She wanders glumly across the room and crumples into her easy chair. "Gimme another drink then, Eg. I'm gonna stay up all night and party with Ralph Fwa Fwa, Ralph Fwa Fwa Motors, in the beautiful city of…what the hell is the name of that city?"

"Teefwafwa."

"Yeaaaah." She squints through a millimeter gap between forefinger and thumb. "Just a little drinky drinky, Eg."

"We gotta go, Pat."

Pat lunges out of the easy chair, snorting and tossing her head. She clips the TV stand with her hip, making a ballet burlesque out of it, hands entwined above her brightly grinning head. "Whyn't you two go on in the bedroom there?" she says with a sudden reckless sweep of the arm.

"Come on, Pat."

"No, no," she says, "I'm not stupid. See?" She gestures from waist to floor, reciting: "Hole in the ground, ass, hole in the ground, ass…." Then she begins to drum the wall with her fist. "But I'll never be alone as long as I've got my *friends*."

"Can we go, Edgar?"

Pat struggles to put a record on, Creedence Clearwater Revival, her favorite in the *world*. Her face is peaceful now as she dances sloppily about the room, staring at us like a two-year-old who has just learned to walk. She catches Norma around the waist and drags her out onto floor. Norma follows, rolling her eyes.

Then the two are sitting on the couch, Pat's arm around her. "Norma, Norma, Chlormaforma, my pers'nul anathezh – I can't say that. How do you say that? What the hell – shit on the lips." She throws her head back and cackles madly. "Everybody loves Norma. Except Easter Egbert. He's going *surf*ing in the morning. But I love Norma," she sighs, her voice trailing off. "She's my beautiful buddy, my beautiful buddy…"

"O K, Pat," I say. "We have to go now."

Pat seems to forget that I am in the room. She is whispering the word "baby" into Norma's ear and rubbing the inside of her leg.

Norma's face has turned to marble.

"O K, Pat," I say. "That's enough now."

Pat, lathered and huffing like a train, grabs Norma's waist and hauls her down onto the couch.

I leap sharply into the fray and grab one of Norma's hands and try to drag her out. "Enough, Pat!" I shout.

Pat pops up out of that couch with such quickness and agility for a big drunken woman who never exercises that it startles me. She roars and stomps, cleaning a row of books off of a shelf and hurling a lamp that shatters against the opposite wall. The needle on the record goes skittering across "Who'll Stop the Rain."

Norma slips behind me. I don't stand a chance in any physical contest against Pat unless maybe it is the fifty-yard dash for my life. I can see the headline in tomorrow's paper: *La Mesa Teen Strangled by Crazy Nurse's Aide.*

"We're going, Pat."

Pat teeters before me, swollen and black with rage. She begins to croak demonically and swing her arms.

Norma and I head for the door. The sputtering red demon stalks after us stiff-legged and huffing. She rips the front door off one of its hinges and punches a hole in the plaster as we hurry out, past the curious heads poking out into the corridor, and down the stairs at last to safety.

16.

MR. CLOSE IS A CHRONIC PUKER WHO LAUNCHES LEMONY WHITE lunch every time you turn him. Tonight I'm running late and before I switch on the light in his room, I can smell his sour-catch signature in the air. Disgusted, I rake the curtain aside and snap on his bedside lamp. Mr. Close is a big rubber doll of a man with a paralyzed mouth in the shape of a bent trumpet part; his left arm is clamped in a withered Roman salute against his chest. I dread Mr. Close and the endless volume of his vomit. He grunts and honks at me urgently, pointing his finger. The front of his bed shirt and his sheets are sopped with puke. I am the type of person who when he sees and smells the gag is inclined to gag himself. If I were not in love with Norma now I would be giving my farewell to society from the rail of a steam freighter bound for Australia.

I drop the near bedrail, strip his bedclothes, and push him against the opposite rail, where he immediately clutches a bar and begins to retch over the side. Holding my nose and periodically crossing my eyes to keep the flap over my stomach closed, I think about Norma, whom I have been seeing every night since the housebreaking party with Pat. I can't thank Pat enough for ransacking her apartment and trying to steal Norma from me. How better to cement a bond than to save your date from getting crushed on the couch by an amorous Blackfoot Indian girl? Best of all, Pat does not remember what happened – classic blackout profile – though how she explains the wreckage to herself the morning after, I couldn't begin to tell you.

Mr. Close barfs as I roll him south. He barfs again to the north, honking at me all the while and jabbing his finger at the air. I don't change his sheets; I just roll him back and forth until he's empty. By the time I have clean linen under him, his face scrubbed, fresh bedclothes buttoned to his chin, floor mopped, laundry bagged, and my hands washed thoroughly three times with pHisoHex, I'm ten minutes late to check out. The Administrator doesn't like unauthorized overtime (*well then don't admit chronic vomiters*). I'm the last one out. The creepy graveyard aides are assembled at the nurse's desk, pallid and ring-eyed, ogling me, coveting my organs and personality, which were both formed by sunlight, a substance wholly alien to them. I hurry past them to the time room and dunk my card down into the clock.

I have only one thing on my mind, Norma Norma Chlormaforma, my every love song on the radio and moon rocket orbiting the stars. I am to meet her at her house in the acre of aromatic gum trees at the foot of Mt. Helix and we're going to drive out to Palisades Park, which Norma has never seen despite its mention in a famous pop song, and then we'll go up the Pacific Coast Highway, where I want to show her a beach lit nocturnally for surfing. She hasn't seen me surf yet. Norma's mother dislikes me, but I plan for this to change. My chief personal goal in life besides complete escape from society is to be loved by all. I am a screw-up but I care about people. I number this, along with making wild crap up, as one of my few great gifts.

Norma has mentioned the possibility of putting me through medical school. Of course, because of my mediocre academic record and weak math skills, I will probably have to get my MD in Venezuela, which is a clash with my Australian Beach Hut Reverie, but who's to say I could not be a poor but dedicated general practitioner living on the semideserted west coast of Australia, surfing and eating coconuts or whatever they have growing on the beach there, among the aborigines with my attractive ivory-skinned wife and golden-haired Shirley Temple look-alike stepdaughter?

In the parking lot, immersed in such fantasies and about to stick my key in my car door, someone slips up behind me and shoves what feels like a pipe in the middle of my back. "Why don't we take a little ride, loser?" he says.

I recognize the voice and cheap cologne of Mike La Rue. I realize I will never receive my MD from a Venezuelan medical school. A panicked little Elmer Fudd ditty starts a circuit around my head: *A hunting we will go, a hunting we will go, high-ho the dewwy-o...*

"Down the hill," he says. "To the parking lot of the burger joint. Hurry it up now before this thing accidentally goes off into your spine."

Bladder tingling, knees like Dippity-Do, I navigate a thin trail down a bank of ice plant. The burger place on the terrace below is closed. I see Mike's '64 Galaxie parked all alone in the corner.

"You drive..." he says, pressing keys into my hand.

Mike's car has slippery blue vinyl seats and a rubber Virgin Mary hanging from the rearview mirror. The steering wheel is as white and thin as whalebone in my fingers. The seats and floor give up a smell like fishermen's boots and pee. The seat is too close to the steering wheel. I slide the key into the ignition and click it up once. A talk station blooms softly on the radio: "...*so what would you do then if the world was perfect...?*"

Well, I'd have a cup of coffee, I think, my hands trembling. *And then I'd probably check the surf report.* I can't see Mike's face. I don't bother to adjust the seat. "I'm not seeing her anymore," I say.

"Start the car, Romeo."

"I'm going with Norma now."

"You're a fag. Come on, start the car. Let's go."

"Where we going?"

"You'll see."

"Where?"

"Just drive."

I ease the shifter into reverse and back down out of the driveway. The city is heartbreakingly quiet and lit silkily by the synthetic gas of fluorescent lamps. The car is smoother than anything I have ever driven. It floats like a feather on air. I remember that Mike is a manager of an auto parts store, and I want to compliment him. I want him to like me because I like his car.

"Take the freeway. East," he says. "Stay in this lane. Turn when I tell you to turn."

I see that there is about a half a tank of gas left. I imagine he will take me to the desert where he will shoot me in the head and leave me to decompose under the watchful eye of the cacti. What feels like a lump of dried chewing gum mars the flatness of the accelerator pedal. My toe wanders around like a worried tongue, feeling for and exploring the lump of gum. I want to use my gift for making people like me. I want to tell him, *Wow, your car is really smooth, man. You must tune it daily and watch that tire pressure like a hawk.*

"Stay in this lane," he growls. "You pass another car like that and I'll paste your pansy face into the window. Understand?"

"I've got to feed Bev's cat—"

"I don't give a fuck about you," he says. "Why do you think I would care about your CAT?"

"You're not gonna kill me, are you?"

"Take this exit."

We sink down into the little town of El Cajon, oh little town of El Cajon, where the summers are blithering hot and the first city planners ran out of ideas before their mules died from thirst at the bottom of the hill. El Cajon is a cow town. The only people who live here are the poor, the ignorant, the drug-addicted, and those who have cows.

We travel east on Main, the edge of the city. Most everything south or east of this is open country, dry and brown, people in cowboy hats waving at you from their broken-down pickup trucks. Horse lives out there somewhere beyond El Cajon, in the even murkier and more Oklahoman province of Lakeside.

Mike has me winding in and out of the same streets. We pass the same Kawasaki place three times. I become encouraged by what seems like indecision. Soon we will drive back to civilization where I can call Norma and tell her everything is all right. Mike will have a few harsh words with me, then club me in the chin. I will have to get stitches, make up a story about slipping and falling on the bathroom sink, but it will be all right, even if I am missing a few teeth, because I will still be alive.

"This is it," he says finally. "Pull up over there. Under that tree."

I am no longer encouraged. "What is this?" I say, scraping the Galaxie's tires along the curb.

"It's where you live. Turn off the car. Gimme the keys. Get out."

Someone forgot to light this part of El Cajon. Or maybe they just lost interest in the spirit of the original designers. I pray for a cop to drive by so I can hop around and wave my arms wildly and scream, but El Cajon has about one cop, the local deputy sheriff, who is probably leaning over the jukebox in the back room of a cathouse or out roping an escaped goat. I flick the car door shut behind me. The air smells of black-eyed peas and a used oil filter and a hint of licorice. Down at the very end of the block an Old Yeller streetlight flickers weakly.

"Up the stairs," he whispers in a snarl, like a glory-drunk pirate, shoving the sawed-off barrel into the small of my back. "Don't try anything funny. Don't make my dreams come true. No one lives here but you…"

Up a flight of concrete stairs we go. This typically cheap and ancient El Cajon apartment building with its iron railings and numbers falling off the doors appears to be abandoned. There was once a swimming pool, now filled in with cement. The post from the diving board is still intact.

"Right down to the end there, cowboy," he says, jabbing me in the back. "Hold up a second…"

He slips around me suddenly to rustle a key into a lock. I think here is my chance for a break if I were not 100 percent chicken liver. He shoves me inside. Lights go up. I'm standing in a stuffy little studio with a hairy plaid loveseat, an easy chair, and a coffee table. Behind a counter to the right is a kitchenette, avocado-green electric range and refrigerator. The carpet is also avocado green. There is a framed Rainy Streets in Paris print on the south wall and an old playbill of some type directly above the loveseat. A small tasseled lamp sits on the end table, shade tilted. My eyes settle on a curtained window along the far wall. To do it right I will have to jump clean through plate glass, body extended, hands outstretched, like diving through the face of a four-foot breaker.

"Go on, boy," he says, urging me with the firearm. "Have a seat."

I fall into the hairy plaid loveseat, which turns out to be more of a vaudevillian foam-rubber clown sofa: my feet go sallying up in the air. I'm sure he'll shoot me, thinking I'm trying to pull a fast one on him. Instead he laughs, chopped bitter dry mustard green laughter.

I feel encouraged again until I note his expression, which is as chopped and bitter green as his laughter. He is wearing a nutty war vet camouflage outfit, his pants tucked in to his jungle boots. I imagine him showering and shaving and putting on his crummy cologne as he makes his plans in front of a steamy mirror to abduct and murder me. There are clumps of hair like squirrels hiding in his ears. He has more hair in his ears, I note, than on his head. The double barrels of his truncated shotgun are pointed directly at my face.

"I rented this last month," he says. "I got it in your name. Got the phone over there in your name. Bought some groceries for you, beer and eggs. You might even have a little mail." He smiles at me. "You're the only tenant. Place kind of run down. Nice place for a suicide. Probably going to condemn it after they hose all your brains off the walls…"

I nod. My teeth feel like wood.

"I decorated the place too," he says. He seems genuinely pleased with himself. "What do you think?"

"I'm not seeing her anymore," I say. "I never–"

"Forget about it," he says. "What's done is done. It'll all be over in a few minutes." He rubs his thumb along the ridge of the bore. "You don't feel like such a hotshot now, do you?"

"No."

"You want anything?"

I lift my head. "What?"

"You know, a last request. Cigarette or something. I want to get this over with."

"A phone call?"

"Smartass."

I pat my chest. "A beer?"

"A beer, yeah. All right. Go on up and get you a beer. And nothing funny, right? I don't mind wasting you myself. No court in the country'd convict me."

I rise unsteadily, my mind racing like the wheel of a Gatling gun filled with blanks. Mike watches me with a relaxed and fiendishly upbeat smirk.

I take out my wallet. "Hey, can I give you some money…?"

"Money?" He almost chokes on a laugh. "How much you got in there?"

"Twenty-seven bucks."

"Twenty-seven BUCKS. Oh, that's good. How much you think my life and family are worth, huh? How much are you gonna buy my happiness for, huh? Twenty-seven BUCKS? Go get your beer, pansy."

I tear off two hits of Clearlight from the foil sheet and shove my wallet back down into the pocket of my uniform whites.

Ants in legion are swarming the counter in the kitchenette. They seem to be in a hurry, as if they sense or know somehow that in a few minutes

I am going to be a big picnic ham. I open the refrigerator, empty except for two Budweisers and a dozen eggs. I uncap one of the beers, quickly scrape the two hits of Clearlight into it, and give it a swirl. The LSD is set in a gelatin matrix. It should dissolve, but the pair of tabs just float there like water bugs on a hot day.

"Will you have a beer with me?" I call from the kitchen.

"No," he says.

"Have one," I coax, entering the room, a beer in each hand. "It's my last beer, for God's sake. I feel like an idiot drinking my last beer on earth all by myself."

"You should feel like an idiot. You are an idiot."

"Yes, I am an idiot. The world's largest idiot." I hold the spiked beer in front of him. "No sense in letting it go to waste. It's already open."

He accepts the bottle and stares at it, as if he can detect those two life-changing chips of amber gelatin. Then he sets it on the table in front of him. I tour the room, sipping my beer. I am not going to dive at that window. Only people in the movies would have success with a stunt like that. It has to be a minimum twelve-foot drop to the street below. And I don't know what's on the other side of the curtain. Wire mesh? Venetian blinds? Maybe it is just curtain over brick. If I hit those curtains like Superman with a running start, I would probably kill myself and save Mike a lot of trouble and he would probably pull a rib muscle laughing. I pretend to study the playbill above the loveseat, a movie poster from *West Side Story*. He still hasn't touched his beer. I hold up my bottle for a toast. "Here's to *West Side Story*."

"What the fuck are you talking about?"

"Great movie. Leonard Bernstein."

"He wasn't in that."

"He wrote the score."

"Do you think I care who wrote the score? Drink your beer."

"I really am an idiot," I say. "A jackass. Worthless."

"Yeah, so what?"

I hold my bottle up again. "Warm night," I say.

Finally, begrudgingly, he gathers up his Bud with a grunt and takes a slug. I study his bottle, the foam-rimmed swirl, the streaks of foam rinsing down the insides of the brown glass. I can't see those little hits in there anymore. He lifts his neck as he swallows, like a thick-necked pigeon. I nod and fall back into the vaudevillian loveseat. He regards the bottle and has another gulp.

I have a gulp too. "Good cold beer," I say. "I love German beer."

"It isn't German," he says.

"I wish we had more."

"Yeah." He coughs a laugh. "I'll run out and get some more." He has one more gulp, licks his lips, then produces a sheet of blank paper from his camouflage jacket and says, "I want you to write a note."

"A note?"

"A suicide note."

"What do you want me to say?"

"Make it short. Say…" He bites his lip. "Say you're a fag and you're tired of living."

"I wouldn't write it that way."

"Well, put it in your words. Say you're a fag, though, and you can't face it. You don't want to tell your folks."

I think for a minute, push the button down on the ballpoint, and scrawl what he says. "Damn it, though," I say. "Wouldn't I say 'homosexual'? Do you have another piece of paper?"

"No, write it on the other side."

"Can I write something to my mom? I want to tell her I love her."

"This ain't a fucking *Christmas* card," he growls with a slash of his hand, his face darkening. "Now finish the note."

"I need to make a confession," I say.

"What?"

"You're Catholic, right?"

"Write the goddamn note."

"I did this horrible thing once. I never told anyone about it before. I need to confess it, please. You must understand. I can't go to my grave with it on my conscience."

He grinds his teeth. His eyes whip side to side. "All right, blab. If it takes longer than five minutes I'm going to shoot you in the face."

I plunge on in a nervous babble: "I have this patient I call the Swamp Lady. She's Helen's roommate. Helen is the Answer Woman. I call her the Answer Woman because she's always got an answer. You can say, 'Why is the sky blue, Helen?' or, 'How many gallons of purple satin latex does it take to paint the London Bridge, Helen?' and she's always got the answer for you. She's like the Oracle at Delphi. You know the Oracle at Delphi predicted that Alexander the Great would conquer the world?"

"Four minutes."

I take a sip of my beer. "Yeah, OK, well, anyway, Helen used to be this rich La Jolla socialite. Now she just walks the halls all day saying 'hutha-hutha-furby-fur,' with a load in her drawers. No diagnosis except some off-the-hook doubletalk about organic brain disorder. You know how the doctors like to sling it."

He nods vaguely.

"Helen Burbank," I say. "Maybe you've seen her picture before in the social pages of the *Tribune*."

He takes a swig of beer. "I never read that section."

"Me neither." I take a sip from my beer too. My mouth is dry and the beer tastes excellent. The first beer you ever drink is wretched, like fermented turnip juice or Mr. Close's vomit in your nostrils, but the last one, trust me, is a buttered pecan waffle. I have to make sure I don't finish it because when it is finished, so am I.

"So anyway," I continue. "Helen Burbank has this roommate, the Swamp Lady. She's a skeleton curled up in a fetal position, you know, like a baby in a womb. She should've been dead long ago but the miracle of modern science keeps her going. No one ever visits her because there's nothing to visit. She doesn't talk or move. She weighs about seventy pounds and she has chin whiskers and three black teeth. She eats pureed food, you know, like baby food, and shits it back out four hours later, just like a baby, except it's black and loose as tar and smells like a swamp. That's why I call her Swamp Lady. We have to keep her hands tied to the rail because she eats and smears it in her hair. She's reached that stage of her life where she enjoys her own feces…"

"Jesus Christ," he says.

I pause. I have another sip of beer and lean back into the hairy plaid vaudevillian loveseat. My five minutes must be up but I notice he has not checked his watch. Each second of my life feels like a jewel the shape of one of the bubbles in my beer. When his face registers the faintest twitch of impatience I begin again: "Well, I came into the room one time and she'd gotten loose from the restraints and she had her crappy fingers in her mouth and she was just snacking away like a kid in the frosting bowl…" I shake my head.

Mike squeezes his eyes in disgust.

"I don't know what got into me," I continue. "I guess I just snapped. I started roughing her up, shaking her by the shoulders like I'm in a bar fight or something. In my own defense I think this is a normal human reaction. You see something that should be dead but isn't and you want to help it along…"

"Tell me about it," he says.

"I mean physically," I say.

"Then what happened?" he says.

"Well, I washed her up finally and changed her, put a fresh pad under her, and tied her hands to the rail again. But on the way out—I don't know what got into me—I grabbed her toe and gave it a twist. I didn't think I'd turned it that hard, but it broke. It sounded like a green tree branch snapping. It was a loud crack. A very disturbing sound. She howled and then came rising up out of that bed like some kind of underwater sea hag, glaring at me, her hands still tied to the rail. She'd never spoken a word to anyone as far as I know since they'd parked her there, but it came out of her mouth as clear as if she was an alcoholic woman sitting next to me in a pensioners' bar and I'd just knocked over her drink. 'You son-of-a-BITCH,' she said."

Mike crinkles a smile. "Scared the shit out of you, huh?"

"Mortified me. Helen was looking over at me and I thought, *God I'm going to hell. Worse than that, I'll be on the news.* I knew the nurses were going to find out. I couldn't report it. I probably should've reported it. But you can't make up a story about how a bedridden woman in the fetal position breaks her toe, so I shut the lights off and left the room."

"They find out?"

"No. The next day she was the same as ever, coiled up and back in her hole. She didn't seem to recognize me. I examined her toe and there was no tissue to swell, just paper skin and osteoporotic bone. You couldn't tell. God, but I felt bad. It was like that time I lost the rectal thermometer in Jimmy Carrow. Jimmy is a vegetable from a car accident, only seventeen years old –"

"Awright, awright. That's enough confessing," he says. "You're stalling now. It's time."

"Can I ask you for one more favor?"

"What is it?"

"I need to feed Bev's cat."

"Who's Bev?"

"She's the nurse's aide that disappeared."

"I never heard of her."

"Yeah, we gave her some really strong LSD, like the stuff I put in your Budweiser about eighteen minutes ago, and she walked away while we were gone at the liquor store, and we haven't seen her since."

He stares at me. He blinks like a wooden ventriloquist's dummy.

"Adrian says she's dead," I continue. "He checked all the morgue records and county hospital admissions, including mental, and Jane Doe, and didn't find anything, except there were two matches on Jane Doe, one of them he didn't see. She could be dead. Pat, you know Pat, Big Pat. Anyway, she says she's still alive. Jackie the Jesus Freak says the angels took her. Amy, who is kind of a dimwit, you know the nice-looking LVN with the perfect ass? Anyway, she thinks Bev started a new life somewhere. I don't know what to think. I think she might've gone somewhere else, too, started her life over, got sick of us coming over all the time and dragging her off to the beach. She just wanted to work and be left alone with her movie stars and the ghost of her brother, I think. Anyway, I'm staying at her place, looking after things, feeding the cat. I had to move in there after you said you knew where I lived. It's one of the reasons no one will believe I rented this place. Because I'm staying at Bev's."

"You put what in my beer?"

"LSD. Two hits. About 1200 micrograms. Twice as much as we gave Bev. A monster dose. I never heard of anyone taking that much, not even the Carlos Castaneda burnouts."

He squints down into the bottle.

"Well, can we go to Bev's?"

"Shut up for a minute."

The gun is no longer pointing at me, I notice, but somewhere off at the ceiling.

"What's gonna happen to me?"

"Depends," I say.

"On what?"

"Well, who knows, I mean the dose you took is like astronomical. Like butter fries and Beelzebub. Frankly, you may just blow all your fuses, end up a zombie in a straitjacket. Maybe you'll end up as one of my patients, but I promise, whatever happens, to never leave the room while the thermometer is in. I've learned my lesson there…"

"What if I just kill you now? Shoot you in your fucking brain?"

"LSD is a very NONAGGRESSIVE drug, Mike. And with your mind and emotions altered as drastically as they are, you might find yourself with me in a closet hugging my dead body, gnawing on one of my bloody arms or something, or who knows, maybe you'll be filled with so much grief and remorse for taking an innocent life you'll press the end of that gun against the roof of your mouth and blow a hole through the stars, like Armrest Hemingway did. You remember, the famous Cuban marlin fisherman?"

He's massaging his temples now. He pinches the bridge of his nose. "Goddamn it, you did put something in my drink, didn't you?"

"I'd just like to add, by the way, how much I admire the way you planned this thing out. All the details. This took a lot of thought and preparation. I can see that maybe you've even enjoyed it. The decoration is, well, let me just say that the place looks like it really belongs to a homosexual. You know, if I can be frank, Chula is a miserable sort of example of a human being, don't you think? Hardly worth dying for. I mean to say, I don't blame you for seeking diversion."

He's gripping the top of his head now, as if his skull has a hinged lid and he's going to pop it open like the hood of a car and scrub his brain in the sink. "Shit, my wife," he says. "Aaah."

"The more you fight it the harder it will get. I'll help you through. You need to understand that I was never interested in Chula, not attracted to her. I never made advances. She threw herself on me. I'm just a stupid eighteen-year-old kid. Don't tell me you wouldn't have done the same thing in my place. Don't tell me you were noble enough when you were eighteen to turn down the beaver when she came grinning bucktoothed at your dam door. I never thought about her being someone's wife. She was just there on my front seat one night, drunk with her dress pulled up over her head."

Mike groans and musses what is left of his hair.

I begin working on the note again, exorcising the song in my head: "Oh, yes, I'm the great bar-*ten*-der, wooh-oooh-wooh-oooh…"

"Fuck the note, you smart-assed little son of a bitch," he says, deranged and desperate-looking now. "You gotta help me. I need to call the hospital."

"Won't do you any good," I say. "Already dissolved into your system. There is no antidote. Nothing you can do but ride it out."

He stares.

"Let's go feed Bev's cat," I say. "Then we'll go to the store and get some beer and we'll talk this thing out, put it in perspective. I'm not a bad person. I have my faults but I'm not evil. I'm an angel compared to some of those nurse's aides. God, you know what Chula did one time to poor little Jimmy? Never mind. Here, give me the keys. You'd better not drive. Pretty soon you won't know where you are anymore. El Cajon might sound like the name of a guy who slams guitars over people's heads. We can go deep-sea fishing in a couple hours if you want. They got those half-day boats that leave at six. Man, I love the ocean when I'm high. You're going to be OK, Mike. All a matter of attitude, eight or nine hours of Mr. Toad and we'll be having hotcakes with scoops of whipped butter and flirting with the waitress at Denny's before you know it…"

He rubs his chin and heaves a long sigh. He looks sadly all about the room. The shotgun lies harmlessly in his lap. His hands clench and unclench and begin to tremble.

"Come on, Mike," I say. "Peace on earth. Let's go get some more beer…"

17.

TO STAY ALERT AND TRY IN SOME RESPECT TO MATCH MIKE'S unstable state of mind, I take a quarter of a tab myself. I want to be able to drive, remember my name, and, if required, order for the both of us from a graveyard-shift waitress without breaking up into melted-faced hysterics.

We agree to leave the shotgun in the El Cajon suicide studio (and if I had a studio like this, I am tempted to tell him, believe me I probably *would* be contemplating suicide). The late night air smells sharply of livestock and glazed donuts. As I head up Main Street to the interstate, Whalebone Steering Wheel of Galaxie in my fingertips, a familiar sunrise palette of chemicals flares along the corona of my brain. The dose seems about right, I estimate, just enough to charge a flashlight battery off the top of my head.

Mike writhes in his seat tugging two-fingered at his collar and glancing in the side mirror as if a giant tarantula has attached itself to the door.

"Slow down, willya?" he says.

"We're sitting at a stop sign."

He wipes a palm down his face. "The trees," he says. "They're melting."

"Your brain is shriveling." I say. "By now the surface of your cerebral cortex looks like the wrinkled pink ass of an Asian snow monkey. Your perceptions are going to change dramatically from this point on. Remember that most of what you see is an illusion. Trees don't melt. People from outer space have no power over you. Insects cannot speak. It's the *iiiind* of the world, but only for a few hours. Guy-bod bly-bess eye-buss eye-ball. If at any point I look like your mother, please do not ask me to make those apple fritters you used to love as a child."

He scrounges around under the seat for a minute, produces a camouflage ball cap, and slaps it petulantly onto his bald head. His voice is pinched with anxiety. "Fuck it," he says. "I'm going mad."

"Don't follow those cheap *Reefer Madness* scripts, Mike," I admonish. "It's only temporary. Be flexible. Relax."

"Are those *Cong*?" he says with a sudden forward lunge of the head.

"King Kong?"

"No, man, *gooks*."

"In this country, Mike, we call them Hare Krishnas."

"No," he says. "It is bats."

The very stern and dry voice on the radio is saying: ... *and Jesus was in the wilderness forty days, tempted by Satan; and he was with the wild beasts; and the angels waited on him* – I push the buttons – *three hostages...partly cloudy today... you ain't nothin' but a* GROUND *hog* – until I find that Skeeter Davis song. We fly all alone down the interstate except for a Porsche on fire on the other side of the fence. Mike taps his foot on the floorboards, flexing his jaw muscles and drawing manic fingertip diagrams on the crowns of his temp-les. Now, as I take the 163 South Exit, he is audibly trying to swallow something, I hope nothing he found in the glove compartment.

"Mike, you OK?"

"Rumph."

"Can you smell the zoo?"

"No," he says. "I feel gooey."

"You need a beer."

The cool highway air is musky and moist with the odor of blighted ivy, juniper berries, and kangaroos or antelopes in estrus defecating among the eucalyptus trees just up the hill. I reproduce the image and voice of every person I know, mother, father, grandparents, Pat, Hutchins, my beloved grief-stricken Norma, and their reactions to the news of my brutal and unjust death. I almost cry at the beauty of their responses. I think of the triumph over temptation by Christ among the beasts. Oh, this night, this magic concatenation of events, has changed me forever I believe, as I pull into the parking lot of a 7-Eleven on Washington Street.

Mike says, "What are we doing here?"

"Buying beer," I say. "Remember?"

"I have to get out of the car?"

"Yeah, I don't know of any liquor stores with drive-up windows except in Logan Heights. Do you want to drive down to the ghetto for beer?"

Sullenly he peels himself away from the front seat. He is already rigid in the shoulders, the vitreous humor in his eyeballs has ossified, and from the way he is keeping his head down, I know perfect strangers must be beginning to look like Richard Nixon and Yoko Ono. Fortunately, there are no other customers in the store. The clerk regards us with glum distrust, though this distinguishes him in no way from any other 7-Eleven clerk.

We slide our purchases onto the counter. "I am Father Donahoe, St. Mary's Catholic Hospital," I say, in introduction, "and this," I add with a sober nod, "is Cardinal La Rue, Third Airborne Division. We are on our way to our first exorcism."

The clerk blinks at me. "With a case of beer?"

"It's for the possessed," I say. "They desiccate easily from all that shouting. Do you sell flamethrowers? Never mind, we'll just take a bag of crushed ice…"

It's already two in the morning by the time I have wheeled through Balboa Park and perched Mike's Galaxie at the top of Hawthorn Street where I stomp down the parking brake and open two beers. From our vantage we can see all of Lindbergh Field and the gleaming ink-black prairie of harbor with its glittering gloomy battleships and diamond candy spangle of Naval and industrial lights beyond.

Mike has spent most of the last hour covering his eyes and muttering about the gooks and the bats. "Why are we stopping here?" he grumbles.

"We're going to watch the planes land," I say. "Have you ever done that before?"

"No."

"It's breathtaking, even without drugs. They'll come screaming down right over the top of us."

He does not seem inspired by the thought. I consider bringing up an article I read two days ago in *Popular Science* about the cesium atom, which pulses exactly 9,192,631,770 times a second. Without them, atomic clocks and therefore space travel and instant powdered orange drink would not be possible. It seems to me a proof of God, though the article mentioned nothing about this. Mike is looking at me through spread fingers as if they are bamboo slats, and I might be a Hare Krishna or a giant rat. I can see that this is no time to introduce the pulse of cesium atoms so I say instead with two loving taps on the steering wheel: "This is one heck of a nice car you've got here, Mike."

"Yeah?"

"It runs like velvet."

He cocks his head at me. One of his eyes appears to be expanding.

"You must tune it up every day," I say. "You must put a stick of butter in the tank every time you fill it up."

He clutches his throat and garbles something about the hospital as a plane comes shrieking overhead, threatening to yank my liver out on a string and shivering the metal roof of the Galaxie like the animal scrotum membrane on a primitive drum. Mike holds grimly to his seat as if there were a rocket leaving the ground under him.

"Watch it, man!" I cry in a shimmer of grins, a bead of pee dampening my briefs. I point out the windshield down the cool and declivitous darkness of Hawthorn Street. "Look at it. How do they D O it, all those graceful tons of steel?"

Mike holds his breath. The plane touches down and shoots like a strobe light arrow between the strips of blinking blue lights.

"Let's get out of here," he rasps. "Please."

"Where?"

"Anywhere. God."

"The trestles in Del Mar are not far."

"Trestles," he hisses, fingers clutching the dashboard, his face in psychotic, brooding darkness under his camouflage hat.

"It's a train bridge high over the ocean. Pat and I used to climb up there all the time, before she started getting afraid of heights…"

"God," he groans, holding his stomach.

"Then there is always the graveyard. Greenwood after dark. Pat doesn't like to go there anymore either. She always sees her mom. Her mother's been dead five years."

"No, man, Jesus Christ," he whispers. "Death."

"How about Mexico then? That's the place for fresh oysters. You can catch crabs down there too, you know. The sailors are pretty good at it…"

"I'm going to lose my MIND," Mike barks at me like a feral pig with mud in its eyes. "Don't you *understand* me?" He begins to vigorously flap his elbows against his sides to demonstrate.

"No," I say. "Mike La Rue, first in flight. It won't happen on my shift." I open him a beer. "Doctor Donahoe says one of these every half hour and you're going to be fine. Your puckered cortex may temporarily be exhibiting some imitative symptoms of schizophrenia, but LSD itself cannot trigger psychosis unless a psychotic predisposition is already in place. I know this because I looked it up in *Psychology Today*. I had to find out if it was possible that Bev lost her mind because of me. But I know she didn't. If either of you had a predisposition for psychoses it would've manifested itself long ago. Do you understand me? You're too *old* to be a nutty bar. Just hold on to the rails and drink your beer. Soon the ride will be over and you'll be home in your dull green living room at the kitchen table with your jigsaw puzzle of the Eiffel Tower. I want you to promise me one thing, though."

"What is it?"

"That you'll watch Captain Kangaroo with me when the sun comes up."

Is he whimpering now? Two hits was a bad idea, I think, like killing a chicken with an elephant gun. Maybe I will have to drive him to the hospital after all. How embarrassing will that be to explain at the admissions desk? I let out the brake and we coast quietly down the hill.

MIKE SITS PLASTERED INTO BEV'S COUCH AS IF HE HAD BEEN SHOT out of a cannon. The ladybugs shifting in patterns make me proud of them for putting on this kind of exhibition for a guy who only a few hours before intended to export my cerebrum to a *West Side Story* movie poster.

"Talk to me, Mike," I say, opening him another beer. "Communication lines are essential in the maintenance of good mental health."

"Bluhh," he says.

He is probably peaking now, I imagine, connecting disparate ideas, reconstructing nursery rhymes, contemplating the origin of the Doobie Brothers. His jaws twitch. His lids flutter as if they are trying to put out the crazy blaze in his eyes. Thank goodness he is drinking beer, I think. "We're almost through the forest," I shout to him. "We're almost to grandmother's house."

He nods and then nods more affirmatively again. The enlarged eye roves about the room with sudden alarm. "Are those bugs?"

"Yes, ladybugs. You ever seen so many in your life?"

"How'd they get here?"

"Reproduction."

"Whose place is this?"

"Bev's."

"Who's she?"

"The aide that disappeared."

It doesn't register. I repeat the story, complete with bloody footprints and the 3 a.m. glimpse of what might have been her stepping into a stranger's car. I hold up the magazine with William Holden on the cover, the blackberry bottle ring still stamped like a bruise on his forehead. "She was a private person, so shy it was hard to get to know her, but I don't think there was an employee at the hospital who didn't admire if not love her. She lived vicariously through movie stars, you know. I'm sure you've heard the expression: 'Beauty is in the eyes of William Holden.'"

Mike stares at me glassily. I retrieve the picture of Bev and her brother from the bedroom and hand it to him. "This is her, touched up, age seventeen. I found out from reading some of the letters she wrote to Deborah Kerr that she was born in Baltimore, though she grew up in a small town called Wye Mills, where George Washington used to grind his flour or something like that."

"She looks like Mr. Potato Head."

"If you knew her you wouldn't say that. Do you know that not one patient ever died on her shift? In twenty years? I've only been there eight months and six people have died on me. Anyway, that's her brother there. His name was Rodney. He was in the Marine Corps too."

"Oh, yeah?" Mike says, vaguely interested now. "What year?"

"I don't know. He was two years older than her. This was about twenty years ago."

"Korea?"

"I don't think so. He died in a motorcycle accident in 1957, two months after he saw Disneyland for the first time."

Mike takes his cap off, crumpling it in his hand. His head is frightfully white, like a great dome of obscenely white wax. I glance at the clock where four ladybugs are riding the hour hand. I realize the futility of translating a life through a photograph. Mike has gone into reflective mode. I imagine he is digesting the tragedy of Bev and her brother or maybe he is suddenly worried about my power as a bad luck charm. Perhaps he is contemplating an oil change. He watches me as if I am a mile away.

"Pat says it's her fault that Bev disappeared," I say, "but it's really mine. Yes, it's true that Pat was the one who gave Bev the LSD, but I was the one who bought and *delivered* it. I was also the one who gave her the tools of persuasion, you know, *Doors of Perception* and all that. I never intended to hurt Bev. God, she was like a jar of honey in an attic full of molasses. You know, she wrote about a hundred letters to Deborah Kerr? I read most of them the other night, everything from the first days here with her brother and struggling to find a job at age seventeen in a strange town to *Bonjour Tristesse* and that nightmare day out on Midway Boulevard. You know, all she ever really wanted was a family, but it wasn't in the cards, so her patients became her children…"

Mike swats at his ear. "Do these ladybugs bite?"

"Yeah, I don't know what they eat. The other day I found just the tail of the cat. But enough about carnivorous insects. Tell me about yourself."

"Me?" He sticks his thumb into his chest. "What do you want to know?"

"What kind of work do you do?"

"I manage the NAPA store on Rosecrans."

"Auto parts."

"Yes."

"Do you like it?"

"No."

"It must have some advantages. Like my job, for instance. Yeah, I empty bed pans for minimum wage, but I am also surrounded by beautiful women in short dresses."

"I stand behind a counter and pull parts all day."

"I don't know much about cars," I say. "Except don't get a paint job from Earl Scheib. I could've done a better job myself with a box of crayons. The thing started chipping after a week. They gave me this little touch-up bottle. They should've given me a touch-up *gallon*, you know what I'm saying? You've seen my car. It looks like they sprayed it with corn flakes…"

Mike smiles. "What do you expect for $29.95?" He lifts a shoulder and sips his beer with complacently pursed lips. "Good paint job's gonna cost you three or four hundred bucks."

"Like I said, I know zip about cars."

"Give me a part," he says, setting his elbow up on a cushion, "and I'll give you the number. Any car. Any brand."

"A car part?"

"Yeah."

"A spark plug then."

"No, a hard one."

"Like what?"

"Like an air filter."

"OK, an air filter."

"For what kind of car?"

"A Ford."

"What model?"

"I don't know. FAIRlane."

"Year?"

"'72."

He rattles off a number, gulping eagerly from his beer, his ears higher than they should be, the bill of his cap creased like a roof gable, his eyes blazing intently. "Gimme another one."

"OK, a uh, a gas cap, '70 Chevy Nova."

We play this game for a while. I strain to name parts. He rattles off numbers.

"Amazing," I say.

"Not one I don't know," he says, holding his beer up and admiring it like it was a bowling trophy.

"What about foreign cars?"

"Nobody wants a foreign car." He shivers his hand at me "Who's gonna tune it for you?"

"The same feeling I have about foreign pianos. Another beer?"

"OK."

"You like this music?"

"Country? Nah. Those are Chula's buttons."

I swing the dial until I hit a doo-wop song.

"Now THAT'S music!" he calls out, snapping his fingers and swinging his head. "Flamingos. Listen to it." He begins to sing along, eyes closed. I am astonished by the vibrant, clear, and earnest quality of his voice. He tips his head and hits the high notes like a choirboy. If I knew the song I would sing along with him and change the words.

A Ritchie Valens song follows, "Donna."

"Now there's a *real* song," says Mike. "That's real music there."

"Don't I know it," I agree. "He wrote it for me."

"Valens?"

"Yup."

"You weren't even born."

"I was two years old. Listen." I sing the chorus, giraffe-necked with out-jutted crooner's lips: "*Oh, Donna-hoe, oh, Donna-hoe…* Our moms met in a Laundromat in L.A. back in '56."

He looks surprised. Then he realizes he is on drugs and I am full of crap. Relief that he will not lose his mind plus the fact that he has finally caught up with my sense of humor combines with the propensity of hallucinogens to put a normal human being into laughing paroxysms over minimally amusing stimuli. I can see the breathless and cathartic giggling spree slithering up behind him, catching him unawares, and wrapping itself around his ribcage like a green anaconda. He wipes at his rapidly blinking eyes and the terrible chuckling momentum begins.

"In a Laundromat, huh?" he squeaks, yanking down on the bill of his cap.

"Yeah. On Sepulveda."

He throws his head back and begins to bark. The barks are broken up by little gasps and squeaks. I begin to laugh at his barking and squeaking, which anyone just entering the room might take for the cruelty of one man watching another choke on an olive pit. Our eyes meet suddenly with a kind of wet panic, and the sight of each other's frantic, helpless expressions and the sudden break of tension send us both hooting off into the boondocks.

"Jesus hoo-hoo and to think," he gasps, "I tried to who-ho-hoo KILL you last night."

"Ho-har-ho-ho," I reply, struggling for air. "And I was going to put all eighteen of those whoa-hoo-har-har ACID tabs in your beer."

"Oh-ho-ho. And I was going to whoa-ho blow your ho-hoo HEAD off!"

"Whoa-ho-ho. And then both of our ho-hee-hoo-hoo heads would've been blown off, hee-how-how-har-hoo-he."

"Oh-go-*goo*." He clutches his sides and squeezes his eyes shut, shivering like a jelly-filled Buddha.

You could say anything now, shoehorn, poopydrawers, wiener dog, or Eisenhower is bald, and we would continue to be provoked into abdominally deep and suffocatingly paralytic gasping cramps. The laughing jag is aggravated by the ladybugs, which have begun to flock comically all around the room as if in choreographed accordance with our boundless jollity. Mike, worse off than me, is bent over now holding his stomach and the gasps have become ragged goose honks. He rips his hat off and whacks his knee with it. "Onnk Onnk," he gasps, his face crimson. "Heeelp!" he cries.

"Swear to God," I say. "Is someone knocking on the door?"

"STOP!"

"No, I'm serious."

"Who?"

"It's the landLORD!" I shout. "We're BUSTED!"

Mike falls off the couch and bumps his head on the coffee table. "Ouch-oh-ho-ho-ho. Hoo-hor-hor-harrr. OH GOD OH LORD. Har-hee…" He is crawling around now, rubbing his forehead and beginning to turn blue. He will laugh to death, I think, if I don't do something. His hilarious death will be on my hands. Too many have already passed on in my care. Never mind who is at the door, I must help him now. Limited by my own paroxysms, I decide to pour a beer over his head.

Under the waterfall of foam, he splutters and snorts, then falls back on the couch in a heap, limp arms outstretched on the cushions, beer dripping into his shirt. "Oh, goddamn it, THANK you. I have not laughed ever that har-hoo-hoo-hard in my LIFE. Oh, my ribs hurt, hoo-hee. I think I may have sprained my ankle." He stands unsteadily, wiping at his eyebrows.

I open the front door, half expecting to see Bev, Pat, or Lord Winston standing out on the stoop, perhaps all three arm in arm doing the can-can, but I am greeted only by the sigh of night and the clean clam and floor polish smell of the pines and the sea. I feel suddenly flooded with vacancy, a human vacuum tingling with pointlessness. The "magic concatenation of events" has vanished. I realize with a shivering glimpse into my future that I will never do anything important in my life. The phone begins to ring again. I grab it, listen to the mingling crackle of taunting voices, then shout into the mouthpiece. "She's not *here*, Rodney."

Mike stares at me as I hang up the phone. "Who's *Rodney?*" he says.

"Bev's brother."

"The dead one?"

"The one and only."

"What did he say?"

"He never says anything."

"Then how do you know it's him?"

"Who else could it be?"

The front door is still open. The blue moonlit clouds billow like evil fairy tales over the rooftops across the street. I don't feel like staying in Bev's apartment anymore. "Let's go ocean fishing, Mike," I say.

"Huh?"

"You been out there?"

"Ocean fishing? No."

"You like to fish?"

"Sure. Yes. I really do."

"They got half day boats at Islandia. Leave at sunup."

"Whew!" he says, mussing his hairs and touching the slowly rising bump on his head. "Why not?"

SEVEN HOURS LATER, AFTER WHAT SEEMS LIKE A MILLENNIUM of slosh and spray on a hot vibrating deck above the great gray rollicking sea hauling God's oddest creatures up from the depths while Mike, my newest friend, slaps me jubilantly on the back and opens another beer, I am home again with an empty wallet in the nostalgic, sprinkler-clicking, azure-hazy suburbs where I grew up. I have a hangover as terrible as an interstate pileup in the fog. Under my arm, wrapped in plastic and butcher paper, is a spiny prehistoric wing-finned sculpin, which seems like the only remnant to have escaped my LSD trip intact. My mother is sitting, legs crossed, on our gold embroidered couch. "What brings you out this way, Edgar?" she says.

"Been a while, I know," I say.

"You look a little weathered. Have you slept?"

"We were looking for Bev all night," I say. "We drove up to Hollywood. We thought we might find her walking the streets there."

"Yes," she says. "Looking for her stars. I was thinking about that very possibility myself. Any luck?"

I shake my head as I sit down at the dining room table. I feel guilty about using Bev as a ruse, but then again how could you explain to your mother that you were almost murdered as the result of an adulterous affair?

"Is there anything to eat?" I say.

"I can make you a sandwich," she says, rising and moving to the kitchen. "We haven't heard from you in weeks," she says, opening the refrigerator.

"I've been busy," I say. "No Miracle Whip."

"I know," she says.

"I should've called."

"You could've. Are you going to stay a night or two?"

"I don't know. I have to work tonight."

"How's everything at Bev's?"

"Fine." I pick up the newspaper and immediately fold back to the obituaries. I check the surf report and the ocean temperature. "I'm getting a bit tired of tuna salad and Top Ramen."

She smiles. A ray of sunlight glances off the knife in her hand. "And how's Norma?"

"Very good."

"She called here the other night, looking for you."

"Yeah, I talked to her." I put the newspaper aside.

"She's an awfully nice girl…" My mother sets before me a thick tongue sandwich on dark rye with Swiss cheese, bread-and-butter pickles, and Heinz 57 sauce. "Milk?"

"Please."

"What do you have there?" she says, peeking at my wrapped fish.

"It's a sculpin," I say, opening the paper to show her.

"My word," she says, retreating with a shudder. "Where did you get that?"

"One of the husbands of the nurse's aides gave it to me," I say, biting into a pickle. "He was with us last night."

"Is it edible?" she calls from the kitchen.

"Only maybe to some kind of blind shark."

"Why did he give it to you?"

"It was that or the barracuda."

"What are you going to do with it?" she says, setting down my glass of milk and returning to the couch to pick up her newest edition of *Smithsonian Magazine*.

"I'll put it in the freezer in the garage," I say, starting in on the second half of my tongue and Swiss. "It's so ugly I hate to throw it away. Maybe I will have it made into a hat."

My mother moans distracted approval.

I call Lemon Acres while she reads and tell them I won't be in tonight, my malaria is flaring up again. I am officially clear of Chula now, but after an eon of never-ending lies I feel filthier and more sinful than ever, so I load up my board and drive to Newbreak Beach, just south of Ratkay Point in the cluster of rocky red coves and beaches scooped out of Sunset Cliffs. The waves are usually good here. The beach is not easily accessed, so the competition for rides is thin. It's a weekday and there are only two other surfers out. The waves, though they are four to five, are not particularly good this afternoon, topped out and breaking in too close, but I stay out anyway and let them batter me until the sun goes down.

PART IV Ventricular Arrhythmia

18.

A WEEK LATER, AFTER CONSECUTIVE NIGHTS PANTING AND groping on the front seat, Norma and I hastily and with mussed hair decide to buy a bottle of champagne and head for the privacy of Bev's place.

I only know of one liquor store, Ed's on Central Avenue, that will sell to me, and the guy who's usually working behind the register is not there. I don't look close to twenty-one and I've already dawdled under too many cold glares, so I retreat out front where Norma is waiting behind the wheel of her idling pale blue VW Beetle.

"No dice," I say. "The guy is not there. Any other ideas?"

"You don't know of any other places?"

"No."

"My sister is out on a date," she says, fiddling with the radio, "or she'd buy it for us."

"Where is she?"

"Jethro Tull concert at the Sports Arena."

"I didn't know you had a sister."

"She's three years older than me. Three times better looking too."

"*No one* is three times better looking than you," I say.

"When you meet her you'll see," she says, flicking her hair off her shoulder.

"Do you want to try to buy? This guy might sell to someone pretty."

"I don't look twenty-one," she says. "Besides, I'm not good at that kind of thing."

"How about Pat?"

"Do you notice how she's always drunk off her butt when we go over there? It's like she's *jealous* or something."

"Well, I have some Scotch back at Bev's place," I say. "Half a bottle that Pat left the other night."

"I was hoping for champagne," she says, tapping her fingers on the wheel.

"Scotch with 7-Up has *bubbles* anyway," I say. "Maybe Bev has some champagne glasses."

"Oh, all right," she sighs. "Better than driving around all night. I have to be home by one."

The closer we get to Bev's house, the more nervous I become. I'm thinking about birth control and what if she looks bad naked or if her breasts are mismatched or dangle from childbirth or what if Rodney starts calling me repeatedly, angry that I have taken his sister's living room in vain. I believe Norma is nervous too. She claps her lashes at me and strains to smile. It's hard to come up with casual things to say.

"If you knew the world was coming to an end," I propose, "and you were going to be the only survivor, would you have all your teeth pulled?"

"Why?"

"Well, there wouldn't be any *dentists*."

"Do I take a left or a right here?"

"Left."

"I don't think I'd want to be the only person left on the earth," she says. "Teeth or no teeth."

"OK, if I sent you to the moon and you could only take five movies with you, what would they be?"

"Why would you send me to the moon?"

At Bev's, I find stemmed glasses in the cupboard, and Norma and I sit together close on the couch, sipping our Scotch and 7-Up and killing the butterflies in front of Johnny Carson.

"What do you think about Scotch and 7-Up?" I say.

"It's revolting," she says, wrinkling her face.

"Chugalug it."

She drains the glass, shivering with the expression of someone who has just tossed off an equivalent amount of hydrogen peroxide. "Aaauugggh. Are there people who really *like* Scotch?"

"I think they're the same ones who like opera," I say, pouring out fresh bubbly. Johnny my old friend says: *When turkeys mate they think of swans.* The crowd roars. Mostly it's the way, I think, Johnny says "mate," clipping the word with his bottom teeth. Though he seems to be having the time of his life, I know he is secretly depressed. He is perhaps the only celebrity alive that I identify with. Norma giggles. This makes it easier to kiss her and in the same motion slip my hand under her blouse and cup her breast.

"Ooh," she says. "Fast Edgar."

We kiss for a while, right through the commercials and into Charles Nelson Reilly.

"Let's go to the bedroom," I whisper.

She tips forward, takes a sip from her glass, and says with arched brows, "Bev's bed? No, we can't do that."

"Where then?"

"I don't know. Not the yard."

I find a blanket and a sheet and throw them on the floor in front of Johnny, who I feel will supervise us wholesomely. The ladybugs begin to rustle. Norma looks down at the floor and says, "I didn't think it would happen so soon."

"Soon?" I say, tossing off my drink. "I thought I would die a virgin."

"Promise you won't think less of me, Edgar."

I peel off her quiet-zippered nurse's aide suit, tripping the hook on her brassiere to prevent a problem later. The perfume slips off her neck in vapors the odor of Apple Jacks and an eager but abstemious librarian who dreams of being a whore. Norma is ample-hipped and has small breasts shaped like party hats. Her panties are the same color as her eyes. The ladybugs whiz around us. The phone blips a ring and stops. Norma's flesh, cool as an orange, tingles on my lips. She looks down with hungry wonder as I take off my pants.

I have read hundreds of articles in pop and girlie magazines about sex and I obediently drag out the foreplay, kissing her belly and armpits. When we finally ease together I am like a pine tree in a valley, straight and tall, reaching for the sun.

"Oh," she says, thrusting her crossed teeth at me. "I didn't know."

The curtain-sifted moonlight and NBC black-and-white signals bathe us as we move. The blanket under us is crawling away like a slow-moving magic carpet. "It's been so *long*," says Norma.

"Blame genetics."

"No, I mean the *time*, silly."

We practically take a lap around the couch. We are that moaning un-quenchable eight-legged beast with the itchy back. The minute hand on the bug-dotted clock staggers along. The sound is off on the television and

Johnny only winces and smiles, puffs from his cigarette, sips with painful hidden diffidence from his mug. Norma, open-mouthed, pushes against my shoulders with her palms as if to keep me from dragging her out the front door. Her expression is innocent and inspired. *Oh, my pastry,* I think, *my pastry,* and then I shudder like the loving baker filling his rows of morning éclairs.

"Is it right, Edgar?" she whispers staring up at me, fingers draping my shoulders.

"Bev won't mind," I say, kissing her damp forehead, her hot eyebrows. "She loves a good romance scene. I'll be Burt Lancaster—"

"That's not what I mean. Never mind. Oh, that was nice."

"Yes."

"How was it for you?"

"Good," I say, flipping over on my back. "Great."

"Really?"

"Better than a seven-foot wave."

She relaxes, tipping her head back. "How many women have you slept with, Edgar?"

"Me? I don't know."

"Ten?"

"No, probably more like seven or eight. Not that I'm counting. How about you?"

"Just you…and my ex."

"Really?"

"Yes." She blinks at the ceiling. "You know what he used to say before we made love?"

"What?"

"Open wide for Chunky."

"Why did you marry him?"

"I was sixteen. My brain was on the front seat. Edgar?"

"Yes."

"Do you like my body?"

"From the first moment."

"I've got a big butt."

"I've got a big nose."

"Whenever I try to lose weight, though, only my boobs get smaller."

"I love your boobs. Really, you're beautiful. You're ice cream. You're absinthe. I don't know why you'd worry."

"What's absinthe?"

"It makes the heart grow fonder."

"You're different from most people, Edgar, do you know that?"

I lean up on an elbow, light a cigarette, and wonder if she owns a plaid parochial skirt that she would volunteer to wear with white knee socks. The *Tonight Show* is over and the *Tomorrow Show* has begun. The host Tom Snyder has that snide crimp in his forehead that suggests to me he has no concept of the suffering and sincere qualities a talk show host must possess in order for people like me to care about him. I reach over and snap off the television. "Why don't you stay the night?" I say.

"No," she says. "I'm already in trouble. Look, it's after one..."

"Might as well stay then."

"No. Angie."

"OK."

"I'll stay another five minutes." She reaches for my cigarette.

A red light pulses in a swirl across the curtains. I hear the squawk of a police radio.

"What is it?" says Norma, pressing a cushion against her throat.

"Cops," I say, heart hammering in my chest. "Probably a neighbor..."

Someone begins drumming on the door.

"Oh, no," says Norma. "They found us."

"Shhh. Must be a mistake."

"No," she says. "I bet my mother called the police."

I'm thinking that maybe they've found Bev. I stagger around pulling up my pants like a man in a three-legged race, and finally answer the door shirtless. A slope-shouldered walrus-looking cop about six-foot-six is standing outside.

"Yes?" I say.

"Good morning, sir," he drawls lugubriously, gesturing with his thumb. "This your VW Bug out here?"

"It's my girlfriend's," I stammer.

"It's parked in front of a driveway. You want to move it?"

"Of course, yes, one moment."

I find the keys while Norma crouches under the blanket whispering that she is not here. The cop follows me across the moonlit yard. Barefoot, I start her car and move it ten feet down the street.

"Not going to cite you this time," he says. "Kind of a dark street. I see you and your girlfriend are busy." He smiles as if I should be amused by getting yanked out of the strawberry patch in the name of an obstructed driveway at one in the morning. "Let's just be more careful in the future." He winks.

I give the Stan Laurel nod.

The cop tilts his ear suddenly to the radio. I hear an address given on Cave Street in La Jolla, the Saag Mansion, home of Nils, my lustrous-haired Nietzsche-loving DICA man.

"Suicide," says the cop dryly.

"Who?" I say.

"Couldn't tell you." He shrugs. "If I don't hear two a night, though, something's wrong." He turns with a backhanded wave. "Goodnight now…"

19.

ON SATURDAY, PAT AND I DRIVE TO OAK HILL IN ESCONDIDO, A small old cemetery built in the pattern of a wagon wheel, for the funeral of Nils Saag. Despite the abundance of large shady trees, it is still hot today, a hundred degrees at least. And even though I have been to only one funeral before in my life, it seems that funerals are always hot, that or it's raining and everyone is standing under a black umbrella. Pat is wearing her tall blue cowboy Stetson and a ripped Chargers football Jersey, Wranglers, and her favorite rattlesnake boots with the lasso piping. We stand at the far edge of the ceremony, trying to look as anonymous as possible. It's hard for me to feel grief over Nils's suicide. Instead I feel dirty and tired. I feel culpable in a way, too. I should've seen the signs—all his talk about the next life and going "on," his floundering romanticism, his bitter retreat, his oceanic self-exile, his cosmic homage to escape – and stopped him somehow.

The turnout for Nils's funeral is light: Nils's bewildered parents, four pallbearers in white with purple-and-white badges on their arms, three blond children in Easter skirts, a pair of bored-looking heads with their center-parted hair in tails. Two women who look like sisters sob silently into lavender handkerchiefs. The priest is a portly man in a surplice with a vermilion hat and a magic wand. His words are snipped and scattered by the wind. The grinding of bees in the blossoms melds agreeably with the swish of faraway traffic. I hear the words "paradise" and "beyond," and think of Australia.

Pat fidgets. She is about as comfortable with death as she is with the ocean, though like all of us, she doesn't mind a peek. I would not have come here had she not insisted. "I don't like funerals," I say for the third time.

"I used to go to funerals all the time on the reservation," she says. "When a Blackfoot dies we buy a big cake from the store and drink for two days. Do you think the casket was open?"

"No," I say. "He shot himself in the head with a .22."

Pat grimaces. "You know, I only met him once and never liked him, but it's still sad. Where are we going to get our DICA now?"

"We still have fifteen and a half hits."

"Fifteen?"

"I gave the other two to Mike, I told you."

"Oh, yeah."

The priest mumbles from his book. One of the handkerchief sisters begins to wail. In my mind I see a FOR SALE sign rattling in the weeds out in front of Saag Mansion.

Pat shakes her head. "Twenty years old. How can you even *know*? I won't make it to forty, though, I bet." She sighs.

"Me neither."

"Where did you meet him anyway?"

"House party in Normal Heights. He had three girls around him and they were all listening to *Physical Graffiti* in one of the bedrooms. I thought he must be a musician, but it turned out he just had good drugs."

Nils's mother is speaking now. I remember her standing at the wet bar in the piano room, shimmering purple ocean behind her, chrome shaker going up and down. She reads stiffly, her voice wavering with emotion:

Our circle is broken
A voice we loved is still
A place is vacant in our hearts
That will never be filled.

"That's so sad," says Pat, dabbing her eyes. "It makes me think of Bev…" She removes her hat and swipes a pudgy hand through her damp hair.

The coffin is being lowered now into the ground. The priest shakes his wand and mumbles.

Pat says, "Nils wasn't religious was he?"

"He was a semi-Buddhist. He talked a lot about the next life."

"Do you think there is one?"

"If there is, he's there."

"Look at his poor mother."

"He was the only child."

"What a waste," says Pat. "He had everything. He should've talked to us. We could've taken him to Tijuana. Fa-fwanna."

A hearse passes. We both turn to watch. I imagine Nils's last black moments in his mansion bedroom overlooking the sea. Then I spy his platinum-headed mother headed toward us across the grass, her face a turmoil of grief behind dark glasses. "Come on, Pat," I whisper. "Let's get out of here. I don't want to talk to her."

"Don't you want to stay for the end?"

"This is the end. Come on, let's go."

Pat shakes her head as she follows, taking out a cigarette and muttering, "I have a feeling this is going to be one hell of a summer."

20.

NORMA AND I DRIVE DOWNTOWN TO PARTY ICE, WHERE THE friendly men in their plastic aprons help me load a fifty-pound block into my trunk from the back dock. I happen to know a couple of these fellows from the summer before, when I worked at the Del Mar Fair. "Don't say anything to them about Eugene O'Neill," I whisper to her off the back of my hand.

Norma is already baffled because I have told her we are going on a picnic to Presidio Park and here we are downtown loading ice into my trunk. "Who's Eugene O'Neill?" she says.

"He wrote *The Iceman Cometh.*"

"Oh," she says, still mystified.

"I worked at the Del Mar Fair last year on the ice crew and whenever anyone saw me coming in my plastic apron with a fifty pound bag of ice in my arms they always said the same thing: 'The Iceman Cometh.' They thought they were being witty or literary or something. It's like when you're painting, you know, and that guy goes by with the grin and yells: 'Hey you missed a spot!' Hey, come over here and I'll paint your *shorts* for you. You know what I'm saying? Come on, people, let's be more original."

"You're right," she says with a self-conscious cringe. "The next time I see a guy carrying ice I'll say: 'Hey, you missed a spot!'"

"That's what I'm talking about."

"So what is the ice for? It's a little large for a cooler, isn't it?"

"It's not for a cooler."

"Then what is it for?"

"You have to guess."

"You're going to give it to War Nurse to help elevate her blood temperature."

"Good guess, but no."

"I give up then."

We hang a right, the ice shifts in the trunk, tipping my tiny Rambler almost over on two wheels, and we shout in unison in nasal imitation of elves in bumper cars: "Weeahaoooooh!"

Presidio Park, rolling green as a piece of transplanted Kentucky, overlooks Old Town, both interstates, and if you stand on your tippy-toes today, the whiffling mist-ruffled sea. I park in the top lot and open the trunk.

"Eventually you are going to tell me what this ice is for," says Norma with hands on hips and furrowed censorious Donna Reed brow.

"I thought you would have guessed by now."

"Huh-uh."

"I'm going to have it set into a ring for your birthday."

Norma sighs.

"All right. All right," I say, lifting out the block and setting it on the ground, careful not to crack it. "You've never gone ice sliding?"

"No, I've never heard of it."

"Well, it's like bobsledding. You know what that is."

"I think I've seen it on *Wild World of Sports* when I only wanted to watch the figure skating."

"Well, ice sliding is the same as bobsledding, except without the bob. And no people from Finland, either." I point down the hill. "You don't go any faster than about a hundred miles an hour."

"Down the hill? It sounds a little crazy to me."

"Thank you."

"But what if we hit a tree?"

"Don't worry about trees. Their barks are worse than their bites. Do you want to drink a little wine first?"

She nibbles the flesh of an index finger. "How do you keep from slipping off?"

"We sit on the towel. Hold on to the sides."

"Oh."

"Here, you sit up front. That way if we crash you can break my fall."

She rolls her eyes at me and hesitantly straddles the block. "Oh my polar ice caps, that's cold."

"It's well-digger's ice," I say. "I wish these things had someplace to hold your drink. Ready?"

"No, not really. Wait. How do you steer?"

"You don't. Push with your legs. Here we GO..."

"WHEEEE!"

"WAAAHHH!"

In a slippery green flash we are at the bottom of the hill, spun around, exhilarated, fallen over one another, Norma laughing. Through the trees I see a half-dressed hippie couple stoned on a blanket under a blue cloud of dope smoke, the girl lying next to her torpid bearded boyfriend with her legs spread and that dark animal patch showing, but I am only the vaguest bit aroused because of the thrill of the ride and the higher cause of romantic love.

Children have begun to gather by the time we push the block back up the hill.

"Where did you get *that?*" says a freckle-stained child tugging at the cling of her orange shorts.

"We bought it out of a machine," I say, "over on the other side of the park."

"Tell them the truth," chides Norma. "You shouldn't lie to children."

"Oh, all right," I say. "There were giants here just a few moments ago and one of them spilled his drink. This is one of the ice cubes. It almost hit us on the head. There are some more down there in the trees."

The children laugh. "Can we ride it?" says the little girl.

"No…Your parents would sue us after you were crippled for life."

"Oh, that's cruel," says Norma.

"You told me to tell them the truth. Come on, let's ride this thing before it melts, said the wicked witch. If there's any left we'll let the children have it…"

Like any good teenage couple deeply absorbed in each other and having frequent casual sex without regard for the consequences, we are damp in the crotch after many rides down the hill and finally we sit on the blanket for our picnic while the children peek at us from behind the trees. The muff of the hippie girl winks unwelcomely in and out of my brain. Norma's exotic picnic basket is full of giant marinated shrimps, a loaf of French bread, nectarines, and a heavily advertised bottle of sweet German wine called Blue Nun.

"I forgot the corkscrew," she says.

"Here." I take out my pocketknife and plunk the cork back down into the bottle.

"You're so resourceful."

"Anything to rescue an asphyxiating nun."

"Here, you first," she says, handing me the bottle. "I forgot glasses too."

I take a slug of wine. I prefer the fresh sweet flavor of this Liebfraumilch over the drier, perfumy wines I'm supposed to like. "Where did you get it?"

"My sister bought it for me."

"When do I get to meet her?"

"Never, I hope. You'd leave me in a minute."

"Yeah, and I'll be the next president of France." I pass the wine. "I've never drunk wine out of a blue bottle before."

"Usually it's green glass."

"The green, green glass of home."

"Who sang that?"

"Engelbert Humperdinck or Tom Jones. I get them confused. I think they're the same guy."

She laughs, returning the bottle. "I went to the doctor yesterday."

"Is something wrong?"

"No, I'm going on the pill."

"Oh," I say, conjuring up the muff of the hippie girl and wanting to slap myself. "Well, that's good."

"We can't keep going like this. I don't want any more kids until I'm married."

I try to think of something to say but the reference to marriage has made my mind go smooth so I hand her the Blue Nun instead. Norma is leaned on one elbow, legs under her sidesaddle, a gauzy smile on her lips. I like the way she drinks from the bottle, heartily but daintily, like a French peasant girl. She seems to understand my reticence on the subject of contraceptives.

"Just one thing," she says, taking a slug from the bottle. "I don't want to be the busybody old-fashioned girlfriend, but I have to know about Chula."

"Long gone," I say. "*Fine.* I'm old-fashioned too."

She nods at me slowly. "I still don't get why you stayed out all night with her husband."

"I told you. He thought I was still seeing Chula."

"So you went FISHING with him?"

"It was one of those nights," I say. "Mornings."

"How long did it take to convince him you weren't seeing Chula anymore?"

"He wanted to talk about some other things, his birthplace, for instance, in Gary, Indiana, and a DI who handled him roughly a couple of times in the locker room as a young recruit. He is not the most skillful communicator."

"No, he is really more of an asshole, isn't he? I don't like the way he treats her or the way he talks about killing gooks in Vietnam like it was some kind of big hunting trip."

"He's not altogether an asshole," I say. "He has a fine singing voice, and he can name any part number off any car, domestic anyway."

"Whoop de doo."

"And he was willing to give up his life for what he believed in."

Norma flicks an ant off her ankle. She seems to be appraising me through the moisture of her overlarge and kaleidoscopic blue eyes. It occurs to me how lucky I am that she got knocked up in high school, because if she had stayed past the tenth grade she probably would've made the cheerleader squad and met the young Ivy Leaguer who would've whisked her away to a tranquil life in Connecticut, and I would've never met her. She bows her head gently. "I trust you," she says.

I hold up the bottle of wine.

"Did you hear about Jimmy?" she says.

"Jimmy Carrow? Yes. Pat told me this morning."

"What's that like?" she says. "Seventeen years old and you die in a convalescent hospital?"

"I would like to think that he never knew what hit him. They say that heaven is eternal youth."

"It still breaks my heart. He was my patient. He was my first one to die."

I tell Norma all about my first one to die, Mrs. Ellen Bradshaw, who had brain cancer and was so optimistic on the day of her admission, but after cobalt treatment lost all her hair and then her appetite and then one day I came in and she was a yellow woman sleeping with her eyes open.

"I had to have help cleaning her up," I tell Norma. "It was horrible. I had gotten to know her and once you know people it's like an illusion that they won't ever die because only people you don't know die. She was like the lady next door. It was very hard, the first one."

"Yes."

"I always thought it was morbid that my father would read the obituaries every morning when I was a kid, but now I read them every morning too. You know, please pass the obituaries. I read them for the same reason he does: to see if I know anyone."

"So do I."

"I keep looking for Bev's name. I'm always afraid of seeing it."

"You won't see it." She tips back the bottle. I know she is only saying this to comfort me. She knows it too, which is why she adds: "I guess eventually we all get our names in the paper."

I look down the hill to see the children pushing one another around on the block of ice. I imagine the hippie couple is making love, if you want to call donking your girl on a blanket in the trees under the influence of cheap grass making love.

"Most of my friends don't even know what death is," I say. "But working at a rest home has lifted the veils for me. I can't look at the world the way they do anymore. I can't talk to them. They think they're going to live forever. They're lost because they see a game with no end. Me, I know. I've watched the people who worked hard all their lives and trusted in their fate stowed away and forgotten like old broken exercise bicycles. But it's not going to happen to me. I don't know what the answer to life is, but I damn sure know what the question should be."

Norma rests her chin in her hand. The Blue Nun is almost gone. "What should it be?" she says, her tongue thickened from the wine.

"The question should be: What do you say on your death bed? Do you look up at the gorgeous nurse's aide with the feathered-back hair and the big blue eyes on your last day on earth and say: I visited Mt. Rushmore and put four dollars in the telescopes? No, you say: I loved. I dared to follow my dreams. I have no regrets."

"That's beautiful, Edgar." She stands suddenly, brushing off her legs.

"Let's not talk anymore. Here, give me your hand. Come on, I feel like taking one more ride down the hill…"

21.

I HAVE TO KEEP CAREFUL TRACK OF MR. LEAVER, MY NEWEST patient, who is fresh off a massive stroke that has left him not only badly paralyzed but frequently disoriented. Unable to use his left leg and arm, he's been hallucinating lately too, seeing camels and puddles of water on his blankets. Mr. Leaver is a soft-spoken, polite old man who does not demand much. From his first day at Lemon Acres he has been a good sport about this whole inevitable nightmare process of falling apart and facing the end. I talked to his granddaughter, who did not remember me from high school, the day they checked him in. The families are always on their best behavior, gathered around gramps, when they admit him into the "home." Later, gradually, the visits begin to tail off. Mr. Leaver's grand-daughter had to be one of the true stunners in the history of Patrick Henry High, where I majored in Invisible (with a minor in Marijuana). I was high on speed the day they checked her grandfather in, so I felt confident with her. She told me his life story, how he'd been an inventory buyer for a cus-todial products company and an expert cuckoo clock maker in his spare time, and how his recipe for pineapple barbeque glaze was coveted the world over. He had a cabin in Alabama where he went during the summers to fish. She loved him, everyone loved him, dear gramps, but they couldn't manage him anymore.

I check Mr. Leaver every hour if I can. But it's been two hours between visits this busy night and as I enter his room in a bit of a rush, I go skating across the floor like Peggy Fleming in a nightmare scene from an early movie by Dr. Seuss. For an instant one knee touches the tiles. The crowd is about to applaud when they see that the knee is suddenly soaked darkly to the skin. Disoriented, I grab a bedrail and steady myself up. I have the impression someone has spilled motor oil all over the floor.

I struggle back through the slippery lake across the room to the light switch, my feet sliding in the soapy slick muck beneath my shoes, and snap on the lights. Mr. Leaver has climbed and jumped or fallen out of his bed. The rails are still up. He lies on the tiles in a bloody muddle, head piled awkwardly into the wall, eyes closed. Gone, I think, but he has a pulse and he makes the slightest of moans. His skull, cracked like a ceramic pot, issues blood in a tributary whose flow was once mighty but now has slowed to a trickle. The shiny dark red floor seems like a great Mediterranean patio at dusk. I stick my head out into the hall and shout down to the desk for help.

In seconds women in white are skating through the blood in a controlled and dreamlike chaos. Hutchins is down on her bony knees in the gore suturing up Mr. Leaver's head and whispering assurances into his ear. Amy is reciting useless bits from the training manual she memorized in order to receive her vocational license six months before. Horse, who works like her name, has appeared with a bucket and two mops to help me clean up the mess. Horse is all muscle and those big lovely dark velvety gentle brown eyes that make you want to give her an apple or a good hard ride around the barn. She wears a very short thin nylon peach-colored skirt and as she bends over to wring the blood out of the mop, her breasts like cones of white milk chocolate in their lacy cups and her breathtaking equine flanks are revealed. I have to keep thinking of Norma over and over in increasingly lascivious settings, parochial outfit, Girl Scout's uniform, Saran Wrap and clothespins…This is futile, so I switch my reverie to the burning white sands of Australia, where Horse immediately greets me sweat-jeweled and four-legged, romping about friskily with tan lines and a whinny…

The blood is endless. I have no real concept of how much a human body can hold. I know from training that the number is around five quarts. But to see it poured across a white tile floor warps the perspective.

Hutchins plucks and draws and plucks and draws, her lips pursed like the closing wound itself. At last with a fancy knot and snip of scissors, she drops her kit down into her smock. "Come on, let's lift him and change his pajamas."

"You're not going to send him to acute?" says Amy.

"He's 'No Heroics,' Amy," says Hutchins, a term that means (because of his age and the debilitating nature of his stroke) that no undue steps will be taken to save or extend his life. The day he leaves this hospital will be the day he leaves this world.

"But he's lost too much blood," Amy objects. "There's thirty stitches at least…"

Hutchins shakes her head.

Horse wheels the mop bucket away for the third time down to the station sink. I lean my head out the door and watch her marvelous backside tick back and forth.

"Mr. Donahoe?'

"Yes?"

"Will you help us lift him into bed?"

"Yes, of course."

"You take his legs. Easy now." Hutchins and I sling the crippled, wrinkled, and nearly bloodless old man back into bed, folding the top sheet over his blanket, regulation six inches. Hutchins is tough and strong for a skinny hippie chick. "We'll have to tie him for at least tonight. We'll call his relatives in the morning…"

Mr. Leaver smiles vaguely at me. I'm certain that he doesn't recognize me, but then he says, "Hello, Ed." I hope that when it is my turn to be broken down and shot off into the horror of the unknown I will have half his dignity. I note there is a big splash of blood like a sunburst up the wall. I'm glad that Mr. Leaver is still alive even though he is not going to be with us much longer. His stitched-up head on the pillow looks like a scarecrow head on a sack of flour. He is mumbling about that cottage in Alabama.

I've got blood in considerable quantities splattered on my white shoes and the trousers of my uniform when I come out of the hospital, and fantasy scenes of horseback riding on the white beaches of Australia are still shining like Deep South Civil War sugar plantations in my mind. I haven't called Norma for two nights: my responsibility seems to be diminishing in proportion to the prospect of permanence. The fact that she has gone on the pill and uttered the word marriage has partly disabled my spontaneity. It's not that I don't love her or think of her often or haven't entertained the notion of marriage myself. I *am* going to call her, probably in the morning before I hit the beach.

It's hot outside, with the overheated scent of ozone and moldering roses and meatloaf with ketchup on the air. Summer is here, though it smells like fall. I have promised myself a strong drink, or two or three. I don't know if Pat will be home, but I'll find her, I know, at her house or Diablo's or Bev's.

But now here is Chula, leaning against my Rambler like some kind of street tough, her teased black hair in two pony tails rigged with rubber bands, the metal lozenges on the temples of her black plastic specs glinting.

"Hey," I call to her from under the hospital eaves. I'm not going to go over there and fool with her. You can't win with crazy people. "What are you doing?"

"Waiting for you," she says.

I swing my head to the right. I can hear the traffic whisking out on Interstate Eight.

"Come over here, baby," she says. "I've got something for you." A gleam of metal appears for a moment in her hand. I have already seen her parading the hospital aisles this evening with one of those disposable scalpels the RNs keep locked away in the med room cupboards.

"No, thanks," I call amicably.

"I'm not going to hurt you," she says. "Stop being such a pussy."

"You are what you eat."

"Hey," she says, getting more comfy against my car door. "If you want a drink, I'll buy you a drink."

"I'm going with Norma now," I say. "You know that."

"So where is she?"

"It's her night off."

"How you gonna get *home*, Edgar?" she says with a sudden chill in her tone.

"I'll walk if I have to."

"And I'll bust out all your windows."

"I'll call your husband."

"Go ahead and call him."

"We're buddies now, you know."

"What did you do to him anyway?"

"We just had a few beers, that's all."

"You kept him out all night. You poisoned his mind."

"We went deep-sea fishing."

"He went to mass last Sunday."

"People change," I say.

"He hasn't been to church in ten years."

"God clobbers us all."

"*Chetos*," she says. "There is no God."

"He'll clobber you too," I say. "You'll be like Helen the Answer Woman after he's through with you."

"I'm not afraid of God—"

Pat's teal-blue Malibu comes bouncing up into the driveway. The headlights rock as she swings around and pulls up along the front of the hospital. Chula squints fiercely, foiled again. I see her sliding back into her pocket the shiny object she had hidden in her hand. Pat climbs out of the car, dressed like a refugee from Knott's Berry Farm. She wears a broken straw hat, huaraches, and a baggy orange-and-green Hawaiian-print shirt.

"Hey," she says, perplexed. "What's going on?"

"Mexican standoff," I say.

"Huh?"

"What are you doing here?" I say.

"I forgot my check," she says. "Do you believe that? I'm wriggling out of my *skin*. It's so *hot* tonight. Why is it so hot? What are you doing over there hiding in the shadows?" she shouts across the lot at Chula. "Come on out of there, you little beaner. Edgar and I are going out to have a drink. Maybe we'll bowl. Is it dime-a-line night tonight at the Frontier?"

"I have to get home," she replies bitterly, glaring at me.

I follow Pat to the hospital doors. "You do a pretty good imitation of the Seventh Cavalry," I tell her, sotto voce.

We have to knock on the glass to be let in. A swarthy graveyard mouse of an RN unlocks the door, all the while staring at Pat the way that children stare at wicked clowns in a parade.

In the cramped little time-clock room with all the sweaters people have forgotten and the wooden mail slots that the Administrator puts irritating memorandums in, Pat can't find her card, to which her check would be attached by paper clip. She strums the rack, muttering to herself. "How come you're not out with Norma tonight?"

"I gave her the night off."

"Bored with her already?"

"You kidding? I *love* her."

"So how come you're with me?"

"Norma and I can't go out *every* night."

"You're bored with her."

"Let's get drunk," I say.

She swats me across the shoulder. "You're a goddamn ball of fire, Egbert. You're my lost Okeechobee brother. You see my check in here anywhere? Maybe they *fired* me."

When we get back outside again, Chula is gone. I inspect my windows and tires and let out a sigh of relief. Pat studies me. "You're not back with her?" she says.

"No, God, no."

"What was she doing then?"

"Waiting for me. She said she might do some work on my car…"

"I'm gonna have a word with that girl." She hitches up her cutoffs. "You know her oldest daughter is *ten*? Chula's old enough to be your mother."

"Are you going to beat her up for me?"

"I never beat up women."

"My whites are all bloody," I say. "I have a change in the car."

"Where we going?" she says.

"Bowling?"

"I don't know."

"Your place?"

"It's too hot."

She is listening to the radio when I climb into her car. I am wearing a loose green sweater and powder blue slacks, sneakers, no socks. The sweater is too hot and I have the sleeves pushed up my arms.

"Shut up," says Pat. "I love this song." Hand to ears, she sings the old Petula Clark classic verbatim. I make up my own version. "*Forget all your rubbers, forget all your chairs…"* When the chorus comes instead of "down-town," we both sing: DON TON.

We exchange wide-eyed looks.

"It's just missing the W's," she says.

"A ghost with a speech impediment," I say.

"Tell me how to get there," she says.

Pat races down the freeway whistling through the eucalyptus trees and hissing under the bat-infested bridges. We park on Sixth Street in a fifty-cent lot. Pat slams the door of her car and looks around. "Where would she be?" she says.

"Beyond me," I say. My eyes scan the windows of the fleabag hotels. "Like Adrian said, if the message came through the board then she is DEAD."

"The board said she is ALIVE. The one who was speaking was DEAD. I think it was Rodney…"

"Marine Corps Recruiting Depot is not far from here."

"Let's go."

"But they wouldn't let us in. It's not downtown anyway. Close, but not downtown."

"Close," says Pat. "But no margarita. Come on, let's get something to drink. I need to think. What do you want?" she says, standing in front of an iron-caged liquor store on Broadway.

"Something cool," I say. "No margarita."

"Wine?"

"Fine."

"Fine wine."

She returns in a moment with two bottles of Rocket Fuel, a grape whis-key designed for winos that would also make a pretty fair carburetor dip. Right up my alley. I want to drink away Nils, Chula, Mr. Leaver, Bev, and Norma, who believes that I am her salvation and that I am really ambitious enough to go to med school.

The freaky people are swimming all around us, the nuts and preachers: a chattering woman who reminds me so much of Helen the Answer Wo-man, a tall hebephrenic marching in a dead straight line like a drum major with his busted pool cue. A swollen old man in an armor of scabs appears to be dead on a bus stop bench. The bums comb the gutters for treasure. The hookers toe the sidewalk in their pretty new shoes. Drunken lonesome sailor boys look longingly in saloon doors. Our brothers, the winos, crouch along the walls like arctic explorers with their bottles of grape-flavored napalm.

"This is so much different from Bozeman," says Pat. "Where do they all come from?"

"They are attracted to the light," I say, taking a sip from my Rocket Fuel, which burns my intestinal linings all the way down to my pylorus, then explodes in my gut with a glorious ache like the grin of a baboon. "Just like we are."

"I only came to find Bev."

"The lights are so bright, you can forget all your rubbers."

"DON TON," she says.

"And life is making you lonely."

"Where could she be?"

"Downtown is a big country."

"We need to talk to the board again. Has Rodney called?"

"Every night."

"Why don't you ask him where she is?"

"If he knew that do you think he'd be calling me?"

"I wish I could talk to him just once."

"I'll give him your number the next time he calls."

"Let's sit down," she says, choosing a bench at the edge of Horton Plaza. She eases her weight into the corner of the moist green slats and tips back her bottle. I can hear it jingle and glug as the syrupy pink gasoline disappears into her gullet. The lights of the three all-night triple-feature dollar theaters crackle above us. Two furtive young men standing by the entrance of the subterranean restrooms look around, exchange glances, shove their lapels up with their thumbs, and scurry down the stairs.

Pat clicks her tongue in disgust.

"Business before pleasure," I say.

"Queers," she says.

A patrol car makes a slow circle around the plaza.

"I hate cops," says Pat. "Do you think Bev is at the movies?"

I look up at the marquee lights. *Bonnie and Clyde* is playing for the last time with *Yellow Submarine*. *Straw Dogs* and *Vanishing Point* are next door at the Plaza. A Kung Fu triple feature is showing over at the Cabrillo. I take a gulp from my bottle and let the flames lick out my nostrils. I am feeling good now. I have forgotten Mr. Leaver, forgotten Chula and Nils. Norma and med school are fading. There is not enough wine in the world to forget Bev. When I speak of her these days I force myself to use the present tense. "She only likes old movies," I say. "You know, Myrna Loy and Tyrone Power…"

"Let's get out of here then."

Across the street we huddle in the dark littered doorway of an old hotel. A gray, massive-eared man in a dingy argyle sweater, who smells like an elephant, slouches past us, grunting acknowledgment. The lobby of the hotel is a washed-out underwater green with faded aqua-green vinyl furniture. A vacancy sign dangles crookedly from the partition next to the desk. One tenant sits with legs crossed, studying the floor under a tractor-sized chandelier frosted with dust. On the chair next to him sits a fly swatter and a *Life* magazine.

As I gaze into the greasy hotel window I am aware that Pat is staring at me, her mouth open. I can feel the heat of her eyes hotter than the grape whiskey. I turn.

"What size collar you wear?" she demands.

"I don't know."

"Fifteen and a half," she says.

"My mom buys my clothes."

"Fifteen and a half, I bet."

"OK."

We stroll up Fifth and then back down Fourth past all the flaming porno shops. The buses gush in their monstrous green rubber-smelling exhaust up and down Broadway. The card rooms empty and fill. The manhole covers trickle up steam. The cops and the Shore Patrol go round and round filling their cages with restless and unloved men. All the pawn and sandwich and jewelry shops have their iron gates drawn. The Pussycat Theater down the street advertises, like some deep undersea creature who lives in

the dark but must lure its prey with a garish bioluminescence: SOROR-
ITY GIRLS IN SODOM. Pat stops for a minute in front of a pawnshop
window and looks in raptly at a purple guitar on display. I can see by the
reflection in the window that she has changed. "You're so full of shit," she
says apropos of nothing and taking a jolt from her bottle of Rocket Fuel.
"Fifteen and a half, I bet."

I have marijuana with me this time, which I keep around now like a
lion trainer with his tranquilizer gun ever since that night, which she
does not remember, when she turned her apartment upside-down. Marijuana is the only substance I know of that will calm her once the transformation has begun.

"I can smell the harbor," she says. "It smells like telephone poles."

"That's the wine," I say.

"We need more wine," she says.

"There aren't any gas stations around," I say. "We'll have to go to the
liquor store."

"Bite my fuzarus," she says, followed by the usual muttering about the
nature and origin of the fuzarus. Deterioration of her hairdo and extended
muttering about the theoretical fuzarus are two strong indicators of the
impending personality change.

"I want to go see the battleships," she announces.

Equipped each with a fresh canister of Rocket Fuel, we march numb-
eared and liquor-grinning across Market Street into the poorly lighted
warehouse district, headed for the harbor.

"The harbor is too far," she says, after walking approximately one block.
"Let's sit down for a minute."

We climb up on a loading dock. Pat takes off her hillbilly hat and waves
it back and forth under her chin. "Jesus, it's hot. I smell chicken. Zip up
your pants. Maybe women don't have a fuzarus…"

"I'm going to write a book someday, a scholarly work, *The Root of the
Fuzarus*."

"You're a goddamn pistol, Eg."

"I'm going to find out what a Hoozus is too. I bet they're related."

She looks me up and down critically, breathing through her nose. Her hair has fallen into matted simian shreds. Even though we are in the dark I can see those cruel lamps kindled in the backs of her eyes. There is a tangible alien spirit in there – brawler, furniture-buster, and girlfriend-stealer – roused from its lair like a werewolf by moonlight. I take out and light a cigarette, making sure the doobie in my pack is ready to go.

"You're a good-looking man," she says.

"The Society for the Blind has nominated me most handsome boy three years running."

She grins at me, leering, her head floating. "You're a pip, Eg."

"People like me when they get to know me."

"Chula wants to kill you."

"Did she say that?"

"You shouldn't have slep' with her. I tried to tell you."

"No, you didn't."

"Chula is crazy. K-R-A-Z-Y. Her hubby is an asshole. A-S-S-"

"I know how it's spelled."

"I was gonna spell it different." She spills some wine down her chin and gazes forlornly into her lap. "You got any more wine?" she says.

"Half a bottle. Careful it doesn't burn a hole in your crotch."

"I already gotta hole in my – you shouldn't wear blue with green you know."

"Why?"

She shrugs massively. "You just don't," she says. "Blue 'n green don't go together."

"I didn't know that."

"Yeah."

"What about the trees and the sky?"

"I'm talking about *fashion*."

"Oh."

"And your socks should match your sweater."

"I'm not wearing any socks."

She peeks down suddenly, kicking her legs. "Shithouse mouse," she says. "I thought you had on brown socks." She sucks a long draft from her bottle, breathing greedily through her nose. I hear the wine clicking as it empties inside her.

She stares at the bottle, holding it out at arm's length. "You gonna marry Norma?"

"Me?" I flick my cigarette butt off into the darkness. "I don't know."

"How come?"

"How come what?"

She wipes the back of her mouth with her wrist. "How come you don't know?"

"I don't know."

"You oughta marry her. You make a nice couple. She loves you. Oh, she is in love with you." She kicks her feet out, bouncing her heels off the cement facing of the dock.

"She's too good for me," I say.

"Oh bullshit on that. We all gotta hole in our crotch. I got two holes, no wait a minute…" The point at which she can entertain herself, as if she is really two personalities, has arrived. She snickers and mutters, counting the holes in her crotch, staring down all the while at my feet: "What shies sue you wear anyway?" she says, taking a swig of her wine. "Eleven, right?"

"Twelve."

"Swear to God? Swear to me to GAAWD?"

"Yeah," I say. "I got big feet."

"You know what that means?"

"It means it's hard to find shoes."

"Noooo. That's not what it means. Know what?"

"What?"

"Chula told me…"

"Told you what."

"You think I don't know."

"I don't care."

"You and Norma, now… you make a good couple. You know that?"

I stare into the werewolf moonlight glowing in the backs of her eyes. My best friend is a stranger to me. Never mind the *fuzarus*. Where does the *personality* come from? Where is it? I have a gulp of my wine.

"Even if you got big feet," she adds, twisting at the waist and flapping her lashes at me like Alice the Goon. I don't know what this means. Maybe she is about to knock me off the dock, I think, with one swipe of the hand. You simply cannot predict her at this stage. What amazes me is how quickly and thoroughly she changes. Slowly I reach toward my cigarette pack for the mari-hoochie, but before I can even get my hand to my pocket, she seizes my head in her hands, like an orangutan grips a coconut before breaking it in half, and kisses me full on the mouth, turning her head side to side, breathing loudly through her nose, and grinding our skulls together. She moans and caresses my hair.

After a good fifteen seconds of this, her hands fall away from my ears and she is staring at me again moonily in the moonlight, her breath scraping across her adenoids, her lips parted in wonder.

I jump off the dock.

Her mouth warps into a grin. "What do you think I am anyway?" she says.

I am glad it is dark because my face is burning. "I thought –"

"Did you think we were just buddies?"

"Well, yeah…"

"HA HA HA. You don't know anything."

"No I don't."

"Come on," she says. "Let's go get some more wine."

22.

THE NEXT AFTERNOON, COMING BACK LATE FROM TOURMALINE Park, my hair still in salty ropes, the waistband of my trunks encrusted with sand, I pull up along the curb behind Winston's dark blue bird-dropping-streaked Chrysler New Yorker. Lord Winston is sitting morosely on Bev's front steps, chin in hand. He stands to greet me, looking haggard. Even his red-and-white Uncle Sam suspenders seem limp.

"Hello, Edgar," he calls. There is a rolled-up newspaper sticking out of his back pocket.

"What's going on?" I say, taking my board down off the rack. "Bad news?"

"Ah, they just put me through the wringer," he says, coming toward me across the lawn, hands in pockets. "Police called me this morning and said they thought they had Bev and wanted me to identify her."

The asphalt is griddle hot on the soles of my bare feet. I mince to the cool grass and switch the board to my right arm, my face still wrinkled in pain. "Yeah?"

"I went down there," he says. "They had this woman who washed up on the beach in a fur coat out by Shelter Island."

"Not Bev."

"No. Not Bev. Dead a week. Green as a tree. God. You ever done that, Edgar, gone to the morgue?"

"No. I saw some autopsy films in hospital training, though. Pretty grim, huh?"

"Grim." He turns his head.

"Nothing grislier than a corpse," I say.

He closes his eyes and rubs the center of his forehead. "You gotta work today?"

"Yeah, three."

He follows me around to the side of the house, where I keep my board hidden. "We're not going to find her," he says. "You know that?"

I slide the board between the house and an old shed full of roof tiles and buckets of tar. I don't say anything. We are standing now gratefully in the cool of the pine shade.

"And if we do we're not going to like it."

"No, probably not," I admit quietly.

He raises his hands from his sides and lets them fall again. "It's been almost ten weeks. They don't come back after ten weeks, Edgar." He swallows and blinks moistly at the sky. "I'm worn pretty thin. I don't know how people deal with things like this."

What do you think it's been like for M E, *the one responsible?* I want to say to him.

He smooths back his pomaded hair with the palm of his hand. "I want to start thinking about moving some of her stuff out. It's killing me looking at it every day. My wife's sister in Temple City said she'd take the cat."

His eyes sweep the ground. "I can't take another trip to the morgue."

I'm nodding, but he isn't looking at me.

"If you want to keep the place, I don't blame you. We'll have to draw up a new rental contract, though. You can pay what Bev paid. I won't charge you security if you want to stay." He removes the newspaper from his back pocket and begins to slap his palm with it. He still hasn't met my eyes.

I kick a pinecone with my big toe. "I'll talk to Pat."

He starts to walk away, still slapping his palm with the newspaper. Then he stops and turns. "I won't be by tomorrow. Or Sunday. I don't know when I'll see you again. Maybe Monday…"

It's already past two o'clock. I've got to take a shower in Bev's weird bathtub with the basket of lavender-ball soap and the rubber swan-handled back brush, and I want to call Pat and tell her about the rent, but first I need to call Norma. It's Friday, her day off. I feel guilty about not having called. I am the Incredible Shrinking Responsibility. But I know she'll understand. She's busy enough with her child. She knows what she means to me, even if I don't tell her every single minute of the day. And I've learned that sometimes it's good to ignore women so they don't think you've become too reliant on them. I can sense the bloom in our future when Norma's mother answers the phone: for once she sounds happy to hear my voice.

"Oh, hello, Edgar," she says.

"Hello, Mrs. Padgett," I say. "Is Norma in?"

"No, Edgar, she went out."

"Can you tell me when she'll be back?"

"Hard to say. Can I take a message?"

"No, uh," I say, staring at my brown bare feet. "Where did she go?"

"She went out on a date."

"A date?"

"Yes."

"With *who*?"

"This charming boy named Adrian. He's going to be a surgeon. I believe he works with you, doesn't he?"

I drive to work along the black roads under the crooked cracked bridges through the plague-stained air, my stomach like a muddy cow placenta stuck with rusty knife blades. I can't see anything but the grizzled hope-lessness these morons all around me call life. I park in the lot at Lemon Acres. The sun is hatefully bright. All the old ones drooling and stinking of neglect sit like bags of rocks in the lobby in their wheelchairs. I ignore a cluster of aides clucking around the bulletin board in the time-clock room. I only want to work, lose myself in work. I know now what it was like for Bev, love lost, nothing left to do but lose yourself. It can't be true. Did Norma contrive this (we used to make *fun* of Adrian)? Is she merely sending me a message? Did she have her eyes on him from the beginning? Or was it all an innocent mistake?

Pat stops me in the corridor of 2B. "Hey, did you hear –" she says. "What's wrong?"

"Norma went out with Adrian."

"When?"

"This afternoon."

"The scumbag," she says, balling her fists. "I'll kill him. I'll make spumoni out of him. Where did he take her?"

"I don't know. I don't care. I have to go…"

I work, but I cannot see. The world I move through is not a hospital with white sheets and the shuffling casualties of time, but Norma's betrayal and my invented images of the two sitting in a park or strolling through a museum or eating spinachy Italian food with some kind of wine I cannot pronounce. Maybe the bastard hypnotized her, I think.

At 5 p.m., frantic with loss and on the brink of tears or of simply dropping everything and walking out the door and down the highway until I get to Vermont, I drop a blue Clinitest tablet into a test tube of Mr. Sigmund's urine. I concentrate carefully, grateful to have something more mentally challenging than the usual pair of soiled bedclothes. I need to determine and record Mr. Sigmund's sugar level. He's one of three diabetics in my care. I have to make sure I'm holding the vial with tongs because in a second the urine will begin to boil and change color and the vial will become very hot.

Jeweled brown hands suddenly encircle my waist. Startled, I whirl about to find Chula grinning at me. I have spilled some of the boiling, colored urine, which continues to bubble and change color caustically on the white tile floor.

"What the hell are you *doing*, Chula?" I scold. "You scared the piss out of me."

"Congratulations!" she cries, squinting joyously at me through her over-laden mascara. "I just heard the news!"

"You made me spill my sample," I grumble. "Now I have to go get Mr. Sigmund to pee again."

"Don't feel bad, Edgar," she says. "It's all for the best. I could've told you that from the start. Rich girls with big asses, ah!" She waves her hand down in reproach. "Have you seen her yet without her makeup?"

"She's free to go out with other people," I reply haughtily, the sickness in my heart spreading down into my stomach and knees. "We're not married."

"The *nalgona* really hurt you, didn't she?"

"I'll be all right."

"Now you know what it feels like." She toes the smoldering patch of colored urine on the floor. "Hey, but think of the good side. Now we can get back together, like before," she says. "It's cool with Mike. He doesn't want me anymore anyway. Did you know he's gay?"

I set the test tube back into its rack. I regret deeply the night I found Chula drunk on my front seat and my failure to either drive her home or call her a cab. If I were not such a morally lazy person I would have never lost Norma. Why did I ignore her for those three days in a row, drinking with Pat every night after work like some common skid-row bum? Was I intentionally trying to lose her?

"You going to the meeting?" Chula says.

"What meeting?"

"The Teamster meeting. Didn't you hear?"

"Teamsters?"

"Yeah. We're going out on strike."

"Who's going out on strike?"

"We are. The nurse's aides."

"Us?"

"Yeah, didn't you read the notice on the bulletin board?"

"No."

"Go read it, dummy. We're getting better wages, sick leave, paid vacation, all that stuff. There's a meeting at the Golden Dragon at one on Thursday. We're all going. You'd better go too."

"Why wouldn't I go too?"

"Because your EX is going to be there," she says, the sneer of joy once again rising in her eyes.

"She's not my ex," I mutter.

Chula laughs and skips out of the room.

23.

THE MEETING FOR P.M. SHIFT NURSE'S AIDES ONLY IS HELD IN the banquet room of the Golden Dragon Chinese Restaurant on the frontage road of Fletcher Parkway only a few blocks away from Lemon Acres. Three International Brotherhood of Teamsters representatives, one of them a sister, greet us warmly at the door and direct us after much firm handshaking, demonstration of dental work, and solid eye contact to a long table furnished with pamphlets, union buttons, and ballpoint pens.

Despite general enthusiasm about overthrowing our evil overlords and dramatically improving our lives, only five out of a possible eleven nurse's aides have shown. After a mandatory employee meeting where the Hospital Administrator warned us that union activity might result in the loss of our jobs, many aides decided that today might be a better day to do laundry or take the kids mini-golfing. Pat scared off the rest with tales of hospital union organization failures in Montana. With less than half the aides in attendance and the surprising condemnation by both Pat and Adrian, I think this plot is bound to fail.

Mr. Southern, a tall graying baritone with a crooked boxer's nose, seems to be in charge. Though he is pleasant enough, we give him the cold shoulder because we know from what Pat has told us that he is going to try to trick us. Pat has watched some of her best friends be changed overnight by these crafty union flimflam artists. At last Mr. Southern checks his watch with a yearning glance at the door, plucks up a packet of pamphlets, and says with a sigh as he rifles through the stack with his thumb, "We might as well begin."

We nod desultorily. I'm working a piece of Bazooka bubble gum. Pat is scowling, ready to give these mercenary jackals a piece of her mind. Chula sits smugly at the head of the table, smoking her Benson and Hedges. Jackie is spaced out and tenderly attentive, eager to misinterpret everything she is told or reframe it in a way that might match a quote from St. Paul in his letter to the Thessalonians. Norma sits as far away from me as possible. She has gone out with Adrian again. I know she is sleeping with him. She is not wearing makeup. Chula is right, she doesn't look that good without makeup, her eyes seem so drab. And she is fat. I never noticed. She practically needs two chairs for that caboose of hers. Humbled by the cheapness of her deed and the obvious mistake she's made, she tries not to meet my eyes. I just hope that unless she wants to be laughed right out of this banquet room she doesn't try to ask me for forgiveness.

Mr. Southern welcomes us to the meeting of the Teamsters Local Number 581. After a small pause he nods and says with a preacherlike snap of the index finger: "Are you earning a fair wage for your job?"

All of us but Pat mumble a reluctant no.

"Are you receiving vacation, sick leave, and holidays?"

Our voices are slightly stronger. "No."

Mr. Southern, taller now, meets each one of our eyes. His voice is firm and paternal, reminding us that we have all been slipping a bit not only in our responsibility to ourselves but to society as a whole. "Do you have a decent health and welfare plan for you and your family?"

"That's a good one," says Chula.

"I don't have a family," says Pat.

"Do you have a proper grievance procedure to resolve differences with your employer?" Mr. Southern continues.

"Are you kidding?" says Jackie.

"How are your working conditions?"

"Lousy," says Chula. "They don't even have a Coke machine in the lunch room."

Mr. Southern nods as if he knew it all along. He has this relaxed and positive modulation of tone that makes me suspect he was once an anesthesiologist. I'm trying to listen to him, but I'm not captivated by labor issues or concerned about my future in the convalescent hospital industry. Also, I wish I had not eaten such a big lunch. I look around drowsily at the garish red velvet walls decorated with golden lions and I begin to daydream about Australia.

Adrian shows up in the middle of the meeting and sits down next to Norma. "I'm not full time," he explains, "but I qualify for the rest." He nods at each of us. I pretend that everything is hunky-dory, even though I'd like to tell him: *Hey, Buddy, Alexander the Great did not conquer the world. He died in* INDIA.

"He's OK," grumbles Pat.

"You're welcome," says Mr. Southern, although I note that there are no handshakes or teeth for Adrian. Only a pamphlet. Maybe Adrian stole one of his girlfriends too.

"Are there any questions at this point?" says Mr. Southern.

We're all silent.

"How about you… Edgar?"

"No questions at this time, your honor," I reply.

Nobody laughs. Southern weathers me pleasantly, turning his wrist for another glance at the watch.

"I have a question," says Jackie, waggling her hand around in the air like a second-grader. "I thought the Teamsters were like truck drivers and stuff like that."

"We represent all labor," Mr. Southern replies with a gentle smile. "Public employees, food workers, nurses. Anyone interested in democratic and fair representation."

"Right on," says Pat sarcastically.

Chula says, "If we vote for the union are our uniforms going to change?"

"No, Chula," says Adrian, "but you will have to learn how to drive a forklift."

"Shut up, Adrian," says Chula.

Norma says, "I'm not even certified. Most of the other aides aren't certified either. I was just wondering…"

"What's she's trying to say," says Adrian, "is aren't unions designed for *skilled* labor?"

Mr. Southern says, "There's no reason why nurse's aides can't have the same representation as garment workers or fruit pickers. As I say—"

"Bullshit," says Pat.

"Are there any MORE questions?" says Mr. Southern.

Adrian taps the edge of his unread pamphlet against the table. "I'm not sure I understand yet why the owners of a small private convalescent hospital would want to turn their employees over to you."

"You just want our union dues," Pat adds belligerently. "You're not interested in what happens to us."

Mr. Southern nods along as if Pat might be agreeing with him.

"It's a racket," Pat insists. "You're going to take our money and we're going to lose our jobs. I've seen it happen twice before in Montana."

Chula chips in: "What happens if we lose our jobs? Can you get us another one?"

Pat, Chula, and Adrian make a formidable and unlikely team, and the Teamster cause seems utterly defeated until Mr. Southern suddenly invites Pat to be the Chairman of the Negotiation Committee for all the nurse's aides at Lemon Acres.

"The *what*?" Pat squawks, flabbergasted.

"Chairman of the Negotiation Committee," Southern repeats, sliding across the table a button with the number of the local printed on it. "Remember," he says to us all, index finger raised, and his voice drones off again into an anesthetic marmalade about the power and wonder of our futures in democracy.

Pat is not listening to Mr. Southern anymore either. She is staring at the union button in front of her the way a carp must stare at a plastic worm.

Mr. Southern begins to explain how much money the hospital will owe us if the union wins the agreement.

"What does that mean?" says Jackie.

"It means you'll get paid retroactively if you go out on strike," says Adrian.

"At the wage agreed on in the contract," Southern adds.

"That's if the contract succeeds," Adrian replies. "Tell them the whole truth, Mr. Southern. Historically, attempts to organize unskilled labor have been abysmally unsuccessful."

Pat, unheeding, continues to stare at her union button. Slowly and wondrously she picks it up and turns it talismanlike in the Chinese banquet room light. Then she actually slides the needle through the fabric of her splash-pattern shirt, too dazzled to note the expressions of contempt all around her.

Adrian mutters with reproach, "You're easy."

Jackie whispers, "Wow."

Southern produces a pen and scribbles into his clipboard, pretending that he hasn't stolen the show. His cohorts sit wordlessly, hands folded confidently on the table before them. I believe they have seen this one already a few times.

Adrian says to Pat, "Remind me not to loan you any money."

"You're going away anyway," Pat barks at him, looking up from her button. "What do you care?"

"I just hate to see disillusioned people lose their jobs," he says. "That's all."

"You call these JOBS?"

"If you had any discipline, you wouldn't need a union."

"Well, we can't all be orthopedic SURGEONS," she spits back at him.

"Management champ one second," Adrian responds. "Cesar Chavez the next."

"Who's Cesar Chavez?" says Jackie.

"The grape guy," says Chula.

Adrian continues to shake his head. Pat, Chairman of the Negotiation Committee and possessor of genuine social power for the first time in her life, glares back.

"All right. All right," Mr. Southern says, hands out like a boxing referee. "Everyone has a right to an opinion. This is a democratic process. We all have an equal voice. Please. There's still quite a bit of business left to attend to. First of all, let's welcome Pat Fillmore here to local 581." He holds out his hand.

The three reps and Jackie spatter their palms in applause. Jackie stops when she sees the rest of us with our hands in our laps.

Terms of the first contract are presented. The strategy to compel our evil overlords to accept our terms is laid. Since management has already formally adopted an antiunion position, our only choice is to strike. It sounds like a paid vacation to me, twenty-five bucks a week for carrying a sign around four hours a day, five days a week, about half of what we would be paid as full-time nurse's aides. We'll get a Teamster card, too, which will assure us a job in case the strike flops.

Pat suddenly thinks it's a great idea to go out on strike.

An oral vote is taken. Three to two we decide to go out on strike. I feel I should vote no, at least on behalf of Bev, who I believe would not want to be numbered among disgruntled meat packers and stevedores, but I am also sick to my stomach from loss, and I don't want to work at Lemon Acres anymore anyway.

Adrian, disgusted with us, rises to leave. Norma follows him. The meeting is adjourned. Pat, starstruck, lingers back with her new pals. I walk to the exit alone and wonder about my premonition not so long ago that I would lose all of my friends.

24.

THREE WEEKS LATER I'M DOZING IN BEV'S CHAIR WITH AN open copy of *Silver Screen*, October 1953, in my lap. It's early afternoon. Pat and I have decided to keep the apartment for a while. We have put the phone and utilities in her name. Even if the statistics indicate that after three months the likelihood of a missing person returning home alive is one in a thousand, we cling to the odds. My Endless Summer Vacation Fund has dwindled to a puff of dust, though as I slumber in my chair, drained and burnt from carrying a placard on a picket line in the hot sun for four hours this morning, I can still dream of Australia, of dark girls and shaggy coconuts and shapely waves. The phone begins to ring. I sit up, rubbing my face, and pick up the receiver, thinking it must be Winston or Pat. It's too early for Rodney.

"Hello?"

"Edgar?" the voice says.

"Yes?"

"Adrian De Persiis Vona."

"Oh, hi Adrian," I reply stiffly, setting the movie magazine aside. Adrian has called me only once before to ask if I would work one of his shifts. "What's up?"

"Not much," he says. "Called to tell you…" He clears his throat. The gravity of his tone leads me to believe he has something important to say. I think for a moment he is going to apologize for stealing Norma from me.

"You alone?" he says.

"Yeah."

"Pat's not there?"

"No."

"Listen." He is quiet for a moment, as if he is about to change his mind. Then he says, "Remember when I told you three months ago about the two postmortem Jane Does that matched Bev's description? One was a junkie and the other one I didn't see?"

I rub my forehead. "I remember."

"Well, I saw the other one," he says. "It was Bev."

My heart stumbles into my ribs. The phone slips in my hand. I know this is not a joke so my only hope is that I am still dreaming. I check the early afternoon sun in the lace designs of Bev's curtains. "Are you sure?"

"No doubt about it."

"Jesus." I stare at the floor. "How?"

"They found her downtown in a room at the Knickerbocker. It's a run-down hotel on Third Street. Rooms by the week."

"I know it. How'd she get there?"

"I thought you might tell me."

"How did she die, Adrian?"

"I can't give you manner or means but ventricular arrhythmia was what they wrote on the warrant. Her heart quit."

"From what?"

"Fright, maybe. I don't know. I thought you might be able to tell me."

"How would I know?"

"You still don't want to tell me, huh?"

"Just because I was the last one to see her doesn't mean I know everything that happened to her after she disappeared..."

"She'd been dead two days," he says. "That means she was unaccounted for seven or eight days. What happened that night, Edgar?"

"We had some drinks," I mumble, noting the parrot crook of my nose as I turn my head. "Pat and I went to the store. When we came back she was gone. We looked for her. That's all there is to it."

"Still don't want to tell me, huh?"

"What difference does it make now? What do you think, Pat and I plotted to *murder* her?"

I can almost hear him nodding on the other end. "You know, I waited four weeks for a toxicology report."

"And?"

"Negative. I would've bet money she was drugged, but she had nothing in her system. She was pretty bruised up. They ID'd her as homeless. That's how we ended up with her."

"We?"

"The university. She was a – subject cadaver."

"For dissection?"

"Yeah, that's all we get, donors and whatever the state doesn't want. It wasn't my idea. Do you think I liked seeing her wheeled into the theater?"

I cross my legs awkwardly. Shadows of fat sparrows flitter across the curtains. "Does anyone else know?"

"No. And I don't think they should. Nothing's going to bring her back, is it?"

"What about the cops?"

"What about them? They dropped the ball. They should've matched her. They don't get anything."

I lean forward suddenly. "So why are you telling me?"

"I heard you and Pat were still paying rent on her apartment. I thought you gave it up last month. If I had known I would've told you sooner. I'm going to New York in three weeks."

I wait for him to say something else, to apologize, to criticize, to recite

Shakespeare or quote that line from the Bible about the dead burying their dead, which I have never understood. I see the students carving Bev up on the steel table, weighing her organs and making jokes. I see her gentle and bruised, pale as cream, wasted in the cheeks, her sad gray eyes still open. I consider the horror of her last days on earth. I consider my role in her fate. *Oh, Bev,* I think. *I murdered you.* The phone is wet in my hands. I feel myself grinning dryly, the blinking mechanism in my eyelids convulsing.

"I'm sorry about all this, Edgar," he says. "I really am."

"Thanks for telling me," I whisper.

"Do her memory a favor and keep it a secret," he says. "You owe her that much."

"Yes."

"I've got to go," he says. "I'll see you around."

25.

A FEW DAYS LATER PAT CALLS ME FROM A REPAIR SHOP ON Jackson Drive. "I need forty bucks," she says. "Or I can't get my car out of the shop."

When I arrive twenty minutes later, Pat's Malibu is still up on the rack and a kid my age is peering perplexedly up the hydraulic pole. I have brought a couple of breakfast beers. Beer has lots of vitamins: B, E, E, and R. I find Pat milling around on the lot, hands in pockets, deep in thought.

"What's wrong with your car?" I say.

"I don't know," she answers absently. "It sounds like there's a whistle going off under the hood."

I offer her one of the breakfast beers.

"No thanks," she says. She hardly smiles. Her hair is so short now she looks like an overweight drill instructor in her sky blue bowling shirt. I haven't seen her much lately, except out on the picket line. She's been busy organizing, and she's taking some evening accounting classes at Grossmont College. I've been spending most of my free time at the beach, surfing and licking my wounds. I rip the tab off of my beer, which is warm but tastes good nevertheless. Morning is the best time for beer, followed closely by afternoon and then there is a tie between evening and night.

"You got the money?" she says.

I hand her the forty bucks. "This is all I have. My savings are officially spent."

"I'll get it back to you."

"No problem," I say.

"I can't afford to pay Bev's rent anymore," she says, folding the money into her front pocket. "We're gonna have to let the place go."

"I know," I say.

"I don't care what Adrian or the police say," she says. "Bev is alive."

"Wherever she is, though," I say. "I don't think she's coming back."

"She'll come back," she replies stubbornly.

"She's been gone over three months," I say quietly. "No ransom note. No postcard from Tahiti." I take a hot gulp from my cidery beer. "She's not coming back."

"What makes you so negative all of a sudden?"

"I don't know. Reality, I guess. I'm not sleeping there anymore. What's the point?"

The Malibu is being lowered now. The kid my age is wiping his hands on a rag. I can see crowded against the back window the placards for local 581, which is about two weeks away from withdrawing its campaign and leaving us out of a job, as Adrian and Pat herself predicted. I finish my beer and toss the can into the trash. The air wafts down in a warm black-pepper vapor from the Kentucky Fried Chicken smokestacks across the street. I open the second beer and wonder what I will have for breakfast now that I am out of money. I am suddenly aware of time, which continues to move, whether you have your act together or not.

"I think we should have a farewell party for her," she says.

"Yes," I say. "Good idea."

"At her house."

"I don't think Winston will mind."

"What are we going to do with all her stuff?"

"Winston's going to put most of it in storage."

"Do you want any of it," she says, "to remember her by?"

I think of the glass syringe, the deer paintings, the ancient radio, the showbiz magazines, letters to Deborah Kerr, a black-and-white TV showing one last run of *The King and I*. But there is nothing I want from Bev, except to see her again.

26.

I WAIT IN BEV'S APARTMENT FOR PARTYGOERS TO ARRIVE. It is a cool evening for July. I warm up the hi-fi, break some ice into a bucket, and mix a pitcher of pineapple juice. I look out the window. I wait for the phone to ring. I sit down on the couch and leaf through one of Bev's movie magazines. This one has a piece about George Reeves, TV Superman, from Woolstock, Iowa, "skilled" amateur boxer and musician, who upstairs, after drinks and painkillers and possibly an affair with an executive's wife and possibly sick of being typecast as the Man of Steel, shot himself mortally in the head only seconds after his wife announced from downstairs: "He's going to shoot himself."

I hope for a big turnout for Bev's farewell, but by nine-thirty, only Pat has shown.

"Where is everyone?" I say.

"I told 'em," she says. "Screw 'em."

"They'll be here," I say, although I don't know whom I should expect. Our union plot has divorced us from all who stay loyal to management, which includes Chula La Rue and the skilled nurses, Amy and Hutchins. Norma has complicated my gastrointestinal illness by going off for two weeks with Adrian to Hawaii, a gift from his parents for graduating *summa cum laude* from UCSD. When they return from Maui he is headed east to New York. I hope she goes with him. I hope to never see her again. Maybe Jackie will come to the party, I think, and we can sit around all night drinking Southern Comfort, smoking ciggies, and arguing about Revelations.

Even though it is cool, I have the curtains and the windows open. I don't know if the memory or ghost of Bev will mind. Rodney has not called since Adrian told me the news about his sister over the phone. I hope they are reunited at last, waltzing through the whirling eternity of some celestial ballroom, or holding hands in that park where all the good people go, or watching *Inherit the Wind* in twilight on the balcony, if that's what she wants, for the forty-seventh time.

Pat mixes Comfy Pineapples with ice cubes in tall glasses in the kitchen. I lean against the counter smoking a Marlboro Red. There are more lady-bugs now than any man could ever count. I haven't had the heart to kill them, either. Maybe they will bring the *next* tenants some good luck.

Pat tours the room, opening cupboards idly. She stops to stare out the window above the sink.

"Well I hope Normie's having fun."

"I'm sure she is."

"Boy, you coulda knocked me over with a feather when I heard the news."

"I'm still in shock."

"I wonder what women see in him. They've got to know they have no future."

"Maybe that's the attraction."

Pat jingles the ice in her drink. "They say it's going to rain tonight."

"The weatherman said," I agree.

"I miss the rain," she says. "It never rains here. I miss the snow too. Let's go sit in the living room. Don't turn on the lights. Find some *music*, will you? This is a party."

We sit in the darkness. The wind in the trees sounds like rain. The phone rings twice, then stops.

Pat stands up and moves to the window. "Who's that across the street?"

"That's the neighbor lady. A nurse. She works graveyards at Alvarado. She's waiting for her cab."

"I thought for a minute –"

"Yeah, so did I when I first saw her."

"She looks like her, though, doesn't she?"

"From far away."

Pat nods, gnawing on her lip. Her face in the streetlight is strained. She finishes her drink and stares at the glass as if it has found its way acciden-tally somehow into her hand.

"What are you going to do when the strike is over?" I say.

She grunts. "They asked me if I wanted to be a *secretary*. I put my ass on the line for them. Take all these night classes. A *secretary*. What about you?"

"I don't know," I say. "Have they got Teamsters in Australia?"

"I think so," she says. "But you better get your withdrawal card, just in case. It only costs fifty cents."

"I'll probably let it expire."

"Life is too complicated," she says. "Do you want another drink?"

I wander over to the open door. It is a thick night that smells of corn tortillas, beef tallow, and rain. The neighbor lady is still standing out on the curb. For a moment I pretend that she is Bev and that everything is as it once was. A taxi turns the corner and coasts up the street. Bev turns and waves good night to me. A little drizzle starts down and begins to sift across the headlights.

27.

THAT FALL I ENROLL IN THREE CLASSES AT GROSSMONT JUNIOR College: elementary physics, political science 101, and art composition, but I drop out after a month. I can't seem to concentrate. I don't have my heart in it. Pat has gone back to Montana without even saying goodbye. I don't blame her for leaving. I've got to make a move here pretty soon myself. I just need some time to figure out what it is. In the meantime, I hang out with the kids in my neighborhood, smoking dope in the catwalk, or looking out over the top of my beer can at the city lights from Cowles Mountain.

When my mother finds some pot in my underwear drawer the day before my nineteenth birthday, she confronts me furiously, shaking the bag at me in the kitchen. "What is this, Edgar?"

"Spaghetti seasoning?"

"It's marijuana. I know what it smells like. Is it yours?"

"No, I was holding it for a guy."

"Don't lie to me."

"All right. It's mine."

"Are you using it regularly? Are you addicted? Tell me the truth. You're not selling drugs, are you?"

I'm more ashamed by my mother's rage at me than I am at being caught. "No."

"How are you ever going to row anywhere, Edgar," she says, drilling me with her pale gray eyes, "if you're sitting in a boat without any oars?" She shakes her head. "No wonder you quit school."

"There are a lot of people who use drugs who finish school," I retort too loudly. "There are a lot of people who use drugs who are like the presidents of companies."

"Name one."

"I don't know of any personally but I've read about them in *Time* magazine. I'll get my stupid degree, don't you worry."

"And what about all the money we wasted on books, art supplies, tuition, and that new Texas Instruments pocket calculator you just had to have for your physics class?"

"I will use the books and the calculator when I go to state university next spring," I inform her grimly. "I'll pay you back for the tuition. It wasn't that much…"

"You're not going next spring," she snaps. "And if you did you wouldn't qualify. Your grades are no good. Your only motivation seems to be to get to the beach."

"I can get into Berkeley with a 2.0."

"You haven't even applied."

"Pot is not that big of a deal, Mom."

"And that's why Nils committed suicide."

"It wasn't pot."

"That's not what Mrs. Saag said when I talked to her. The note specifically mentioned drugs."

I'm not going to give my mother a lecture on street drugs. I don't want to appear to know any more about them than I already do. But it is my firm opinion that if Nils Saag, Karmic Neil Young child of the brilliant architect and last chance purveyor of the "pure," had had to work a summer or two at Jack-in-the-Box or cleaning up society's discarded elderly, he would've never taken his life. He didn't get trapped by drugs but by the illusion of ease and the impenetrability of his feeble idealism up in that eagle's nest bedroom surrounded by his addled heroes and his organic carrots.

She glares at me, the disappointment in her face showing through her anger. "I'm not going to tell your father about this," she says, dumping the bag upside-down over the garbage disposal. "But it's obvious we've given you too much freedom. From now on, as long as you live here you'll live by our rules." She flicks up the switch and shouts over the grinding: "Now if you don't want to go to school and if you're not going to work, I want you in by eleven o'clock. And I don't want you seeing that girl down the street. She's sixteen. You think I don't hear you bringing her down to your room after we've gone to bed? Do you know that's statutory rape?"

I've listened to enough. "I'll move out then!" I shout, on the verge of tears. "I don't need this!" I slam the door after me, vowing never to return. When I get to my car I realize I've left the keys back in my room. Too proud to return, I stomp barefoot out to the boulevard and stick out my thumb. A bubble-top Econoline van swerves over and the door swings out. Jerry Garcia or his furry twin brother, Hairy, leans down. "Where you headed, pard?"

"Beach."

"I'm going down to Garnet, man. PB all right?"

"Perfect."

"All aboard, dude."

Hairy's van has captain's chairs planted into a knee-deep sea of soda cans, Twizzler wrappers, and ripped-up copies of *Guitar* magazine. Quicksilver Messenger Service plays on about eighteen speakers. No matter how good your sound system is, however, Quicksilver Messenger Service always makes your tape player sound like it needs to be cleaned.

"I'm Drover," he says. "My friends call me Drove."

"I'm Edgar," I say. We shake hands soul-brother style.

"What brings you out this way without any shoes?"

"I had a fight with my mom. She accused me of selling dope."

"Bummer," he says. "She shoulda gave you a medal. You want to smoke some honey oil?"

"Cool."

With one hand on the wheel Drover manages to heat a vial of honey oil, which is basically boiled, concentrated marijuana, stronger than hashish, the blackstrap at the bottom of the cannabis vat. He drips the heated oil onto the screen of a pipe shaped like a glass tuba, gets the ball chamber whirling with yellow-black smoke similar to the type you would see pouring from a trash fire, stokes his chest, cracks his nasal barrier trying to hold it down, and passes it across. I gulp down too large a hit and the petroleum-like cloud expands like a time-elapse film of a blossoming rosebush in my lungs and finally discharges itself in convulsive slobbery blasts through all five of my pharyngeal cavities. I cough so long and hard the muscles in the soles of my feet begin to cramp. Drover, exhausted from laughing, finally drops me off somewhere in Pacific Beach with a sunny good luck wave, and I wander down the street, stoned out of my mind, unsure of which city I might be in.

Honey oil is like scaly black lizards with muddy feet that have mistaken your brain for a permanent place to live. I slog along the spongy sidewalk like a basset hound with green slaver hanging from my jowls until I see the beneficent gray shimmer of the Pacific Ocean. The sun is only an hour away from going down. The tourists have all gone home. There is no one out except for a knot of Mexicans drinking cans of malt liquor over by the horseshoe pits, a family packing up their picnic basket, and two scraggly dudes, who I imagine just got off the bus from Syracuse, New York, one with a bad limp, staring pathetically out at their mythical sea.

I amble down the beach. The waves melt and hush in. I wonder where my new home will be. Maybe I will crash on someone's couch tonight and in the morning hitchhike down to Baja and camp on the beach somewhere past Las Escobas for the winter. I could live there for nothing, hole up in a cave in a cliff. I hear one of the Syracuse boys say to his buddy: "Go on in, man. It'll cure your leg."

Before I get to the pier I have stripped to my boxers, left my clothes in a pile, and dived into the sea. The water is warm as wool. As the air temp drops the water softens and the waves, their shape improved by the breeze drawn from the cooling shore, break so even and clean I can take three strokes and sit in the collar of the curl, cut the wave face like a diamond across glass, the foam chasing me like a flock of maimed geese or a benediction of whipped cream. I duck in and out of the surf like a seal, restoring my balance, cleaning the lizard cage of my brain.

Fall is clam season. I can't resist clawing through the soup and scooping after the scuttling bivalves. I pull up orange and green and gray clams with purple bands. Some of them are as big as my fist. And though you can steam them in a coffee can with seawater over a beach fire and eat them with butter, I throw them back because I don't have a coffee can or any butter and anyway I am too stoned.

A ribbon of orange smoke clings to the horizon and the caps and veins of spume in the waves have begun to glow by the time I finally climb out of the water. The air temperature has plunged. A few stars have wiggled out to burn tenuously in the pearl dusky sky. Most of the lights in the cottages up on the pier are on. I look for my clothes. Oh, this is good, too high to remember where I put my clothes. I travel around in a futile, chattering circle. After a few minutes, I realize my clothes have been stolen. The clothes are of no particular value to me (though I still cling to customs of wearing them in public), but my wallet was among them, driver's license, Teamsters Union withdrawal card, social security card, fifteen and a half hits of Clearlight, and about seven dollars in cash.

A guy who looks like a schoolteacher is standing at the head of the beach with hands in pockets, staring at me. I think for a minute he might be the joker responsible. I stroll up the sand, making an effort to keep the flap in the front of my boxers from gaping.

"You're Edgar Donahoe," he says.

"Yeah, should I know you?"

"You took care of my mother."

"Who?"

"Bradshaw. Ellen Bradshaw."

"Oh, yes, Mrs. Bradshaw."

"I always intended to thank you people at Lemon Acres, write you a card – you were all so kind. My mother spoke particularly well of you."

He grips the left lens of his wire-rimmed spectacles. "But when she died, well, I…"

I try not to think of Lemon Acres anymore. It reminds me of all the people I have lost that I know are never coming back. I shiver in my underwear. "You don't need to thank me," I say. "It's not that kind of a job."

"Are you still there?" he says.

"No, I quit. There was a strike."

"That's too bad," he says.

"I hate to ask you this," I say, "but someone stole my clothes and I need a dime to make a phone call."

"Of course," he says, digging into his pocket. "Can I give you a ride somewhere?"

"No, I'll be all right."

He places the dime in my palm. "Well, good luck," he says.

I thank him and walk away, wondering who to call.

Titles available from Hawthorne Books

AT YOUR LOCAL BOOKSELLER OR FROM OUR WEBSITE: *hawthornebooks.com*

Saving Stanley: The Brickman Stories
BY SCOTT NADELSON

This debut collection of interrelated short stories are graceful, vivid narratives that bring into sudden focus the spirit and the stubborn resilience of the Brickmans, a Jewish family of four living in suburban New Jersey. The central character, Daniel Brickman, forges obstinately through his own plots and desires as he struggles to balance his sense of identity with his longing to gain acceptance from his family and peers. This fierce collection provides an unblinking examination of family life and the human instinct for attachment.

SCOTT NADELSON PLAYFULLY INTRODUCES *us to a fascinating family of characters with sharp and entertaining psychological observations in gracefully beautiful language, reminiscent of young Updike. I wish I could write such sentences. There is a lot of eros and humor here – a perfectly enjoyable book.*
　　　　　　　　　　　　　　　　　　　　—JOSIP NOVAKOVICH
　　　　　　　　　　　　　　　　　　author of *Salvation and Other Disasters*

So Late, So Soon
BY D'ARCY FALLON

This memoir offers an irreverent, fly-on-the-wall view of the Lighthouse Ranch, the Christian commune D'Arcy Fallon called home for three years in the mid-1970s. At eighteen years old, when life's questions overwhelmed her and reconciling her family past with her future seemed impossible, she accidentally came upon the Ranch during a hitchhike gone awry. Perched on a windswept bluff in Loleta, a dozen miles from anywhere in Northern California, this community of lost and found twentysomethings lured her in with promises of abounding love, spiritual serenity, and a hardy, pioneer existence. What she didn't count on was the fog.

I FOUND FALLON'S STORY *fascinating, as will anyone who has ever wondered about the role women play in fundamental religious sects. What would draw an otherwise independent woman to a life of menial labor and subservience? Fallon's answer is this story, both an inside look at 70s commune life and a funny, irreverent, poignant coming of age.* —JUDY BLUNT
　　　　　　　　　　　　　　　　　　　　　author of *Breaking Clean*

HAWTHORNE BOOKS & LITERARY ARTS :: *Portland, Oregon*

God Clobbers Us All

BY POE BALLANTINE

Set against the dilapidated halls of a San Diego rest home in the 1970s, God Clobbers Us All is the shimmering, hysterical, and melancholy story of eighteen-year-old surfer-boy orderly Edgar Donahoe's struggles with friendship, death, and an ill-advised affair with the wife of a maladjusted war veteran. All of Edgar's problems become mundane, however, when he and his lesbian Blackfoot nurse's aide best friend, Pat Fillmore, become responsible for the disappearance of their fellow worker after an LSD party gone awry. God Clobbers Us All is guaranteed to satisfy longtime Ballantine fans as well as convert those lucky enough to be discovering his work for the first time.

Things I Like About America

BY POE BALLANTINE

These risky, personal essays are populated with odd jobs, eccentric characters, boarding houses, buses, and beer. Ballantine takes us along on his Greyhound journey through small-town America, exploring what it means to be human. Written with piercing intimacy and self-effacing humor, Ballantine's writings provide entertainment, social commentary, and completely compelling slices of life.

IN HIS SEARCH *for the real America, Poe Ballantine reminds me of the legendary musk deer, who wanders from valley to valley and hilltop to hilltop searching for the source of the intoxicating musk fragrance that actually comes from him. Along the way, he writes some of the best prose I've ever read.* —SY SAFRANSKY
Editor, *The Sun*

September 11:
West Coast Writers Approach Ground Zero

EDITED BY JEFF MEYERS

The myriad repercussions and varied and often contradictory responses to the acts of terrorism perpetuated on September 11, 2001 have inspired thirty-four West Coast writers to come together in their attempts to make meaning from chaos. By virtue of history and geography, the West Coast has developed a community different from that of the East, but ultimately shared experiences bridge the distinctions in provocative and heartening ways. Jeff Meyers anthologizes the voices of American writers as history unfolds and the country braces, mourns, and rebuilds.

CONTRIBUTORS INCLUDE: *Diana Abu-Jaber, T. C. Boyle, Michael Byers, Tom Clark, Joshua Clover, Peter Coyote, John Daniel, Harlan Ellison, Lawrence Ferlinghetti, Amy Gerstler, Lawrence Grobel, Ehud Havazelet, Ken Kesey, Maxine Hong Kingston, Stacey Levine, Tom Spanbauer, Primus St. John, Sallie Tisdale, Alice Walker, and many others.*

 HAWTHORNE BOOKS & LITERARY ARTS :: Portland, Oregon

A Walkabout Home

BY STEPHANIE ROSE BIRD

The American mystical practice of Hoodoo seeped into Stephanie Rose Bird's consciousness before she even knew its name. During her childhood, she took long walks amidst the lush green landscape of Southern New Jersey – a landscape bounded by the wetlands, the Pine Barrens, the Atlantic Ocean, and a rich tradition of folklore. The power of this walking – of these human foot tracks – has been the subject of many incantations, chants, and songs. The folkloric tradition pays careful attention to the cleansing of pathways, especially the pathway home. Steeped in these worlds, *A Walkabout Home* tells the story of an African American writer and artist raised in the Pine Barrens of New Jersey who has traveled the globe in search of art and home.

In the end, Bird is not one to shy away from the harder questions in life. On nearly every page her words here seem to ask, indirectly and in just so many words: Who am I? Why am I as I am? What has formed me? But because of Bird's travel across cultures and continents, the book's ultimate subject is the way these questions provide a connection between people. A Walkabout Home *is an eloquent bridge across the span of human experience.*

—MICHAEL FALLON
Annuals Editor, Llewellyn Publications

Dastgah: Diary of a Headtrip

BY MARK MORDUE

From India to Paris, Iran to New York, Australian award-winning journalist Mark Mordue chronicles his year long world trip with his girlfriend, Lisa Nicol. Mordue explores countries most Americans never see as well as issues of world citizenship in the 21st century.

I just took a trip around the world in one go, first zigzagging my way through this incredible book, and finally, almost feverishly, making sure I hadn't missed out on a chapter along the way. I'm not sure what I'd call it now: A road movie of the mind, a diary, a love story, a new version of the subterranean homesick and wanderlust blues – anyway, it's a great ride. Paul Bowles and Kerouac are in the back, and Mark Mordue has taken over the wheel of that pickup truck from Bruce Chatwin, who's dozing in the passenger seat. —WIM WENDERS
Director of *Paris, Texas; Wings of Desire;*
and *The Buena Vista Social Club*

www.hawthornebooks.com